BITTER CREEK

After four bitter war years, Clyde Cassel rode home to Bitter Creek, minus an arm, to find his ranch gone and his girl taken by another man. The townspeople, plagued by conscience, decided to give him a break. When the unofficial 'boss' made him their first-ever marshal, even the gamblers and gunslingers smiled and agreed. How could a one-armed man hurt anyone? But with the star pinned to his chest Clyde Cassel started a new kind of war . . .

BITTER CREEK

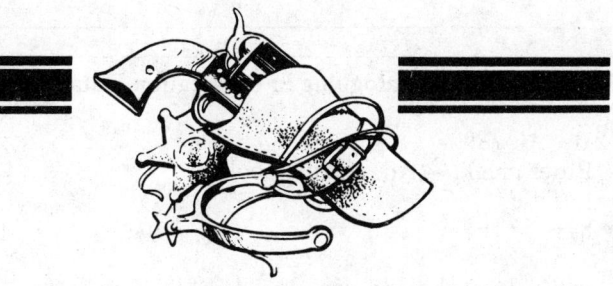

Al Cody

ATLANTIC LARGE PRINT
Chivers Press, Bath, England.
Curley Publishing, Inc.,
South Yarmouth, Mass., USA.

Library of Congress Cataloging-in-Publication Data

Cody, Al, 1899–
 Bitter Creek / Al Cody.
  p.   cm.—(Atlantic large print)
 ISBN 0–7927–0007–4 (lg. print)
 1. Large type books. I Title.
[PS3519.O712B5 1989]
813'.54—dc20   89–34869
                                                    CIP

British Library Cataloguing in Publication Data

Cody, Al, *1899–*
 Bitter creek.—(An Atlantic book).
 I. Title
 813'.52 [F]

 ISBN 0–7451–9578–4
 ISBN 0–7451–9590–3 pbk

This Large Print edition is published by Chivers Press, England, and Curley Publishing, Inc, U.S.A. 1989

Published by arrangement with Donald MacCampbell, Inc

U.K. Hardback ISBN 0 7451 9578 4
U.K. Softback ISBN 0 7451 9590 3
U.S.A. Softback ISBN 0 7927 0007 4

Copyright, 1946, 1947, by Dodd, Mead and Company, Inc

BITTER CREEK

CHAPTER ONE

Sunlight capped the knoll like filtered fog. It had the soft, hazy quality of late summer, and the gossamer thread of it was in the air. It picked out with odd distinctness the deep blue of service-berries, with here and there a deep red blush remaining, or showed the ripe purple of clustered chokeberries hanging low. With a pitiless clarity it showed the old, battered army service hat which sat on the over-long black hair of the man in the saddle, seated statuesque for a few moments here at the brow of the hill. It revealed the sloping shoulders, the lean, powerful lines of him, showed as well the rather tired face beneath the hat, the full black beard and moustache, now in need of a little trimming.

And it gave an added whiteness to the piece of linen paper which he held in his hand, causing the staringly black ink to reflect back more strongly. Not that such added illumination was needed. Slowly, with a sort of grim finality, he crumpled the letter in his hand, allowed it to drop to the ground. The words were graven on his brain:

'It was all a mistake in the first place. I see that now. We never really loved each other. I was fascinated by you because you are a strong, ruthless man, Clyde Cassel—and I mistook that for love. But because you are strong, utterly competent, you have no need of a woman—least of all of me.'

There had been more—half apology, half explanation. He had come through the war, and she had waited to see if he did—waited to see if there might be any obligation such as some women had. But she knew now that he was returning to Bitter Creek, and that she had nothing to give him. So that, the letter had said in essence, was that.

Briefly, almost as a postscript, she had added that, by the time he received the letter, she would be Mrs. Robert Yoder.

And that, Cassel knew, his face bleak, was the gist of the whole thing. Yoder was twenty-seven today. He knew that with certainty, for it was his twenty-seventh birthday also. But for four years he had been away, campaigning—Shiloh, Vicksburg, Bloody Run—they were names graven in his mind, like blood on his heart. Four years, and that meant that Tincup—beggar's brand—would be run down and poorer even than when he had set forth for the wars. It had held great potentialities, had Tincup, but now there would be little else.

With Horseshoe it would be a different story. As good a ranch as Tincup to begin with, Yoder had built it up during those four years. Years in which beef had been at premium prices, years in which to grow. Horseshoe would be a rich spread now, Robert Yoder a rich man. So Anticlea was Mrs. Robert Yoder.

It was as simple as that. Once he would have found it incomprehensible, that a woman could do this to a man she had professed to love. Or that Anticlea could do it at all—Anticlea, with the face of an angel and the figure of a goddess, who had promised so passionately to wait for him, to be always faithful.

Yet it was simple. Somehow the years had made most things that way. There were two verities—life and death. Beyond that he knew of none. There were friends who would betray you, or their country, for gold. And starving men would knife you in the back for a crust. He had lost his illusions, Cassel saw now, one by one, down the black and bitter years. He had kept only the one—that love of woman was a third eternal verity.

His lip twisted bitterly. He should have known better. There were only two—life and death. A man lived if he was strong, or died if he was weak—or a fool. What had she said? That he was competent, and strong. A ruthless man.

And she had said that she had waited, but that now he was returning, and there was no obligation. Cassel smiled, bleakly, and clucked to his horse. From the brow of the next hill he'd be able to see Tincup—beggar's brand.

It was Yoder who had first dubbed it that, back a dozen years ago. Well, Yoder had been right. Just as, having Horseshoe, he'd always been lucky. Now he had Anticlea. Maybe he was lucky. A fool for luck. Or maybe, this time, just a fool.

A second time he pulled up, horse and rider outlined against the horizon, curiously like one figure. There was no great hurry, and he intended to savour this moment. He had dreamed of it for months, ranking it second only in anticipation to seeing Anticlea again. His first glimpse of home.

The hills still lay rumpled before him, the valleys were patches of green in the bottoms, brown on the slopes. Here and there, on the heights, early frost had touched a bush, turning it to gold. Hazy with distance, a faint silver thread, was Bitter Creek—running through the middle of Tincup. Someone had misnamed its waters, for it was sweet, spring-fed, full-running even at this season. A little sigh came from Cassel's tight lips, though he was unconscious of it.

Here and there, as he rode forward, he saw cattle grazing—fat, sleek cattle. He had come north and west again by way of the railroad which had pushed to Dodge and beyond.

Down there, now, were cattle in a brown flood, a thickening stream pushing up from Texas. Long-horned stock which mostly got as far as Dodge, then were abruptly sucked in by the cattle cars.

He had seen plenty of them, an occasional herd tentatively pushing on past the line of steel rails, venturing towards new pasture. Sooner or later, now that the war was over, they'd be coming clear to Montana.

None of them had reached here yet. These cattle had come in from Oregon and California, a few years back. His father, Sam Cassel, had turned from trapping and fur trading, with vision to see that the untouched frontier would not long remain so. He had been one of the first to acquire a ranch, taking his pick of the country. Tincup had all the natural possibilities. And Sam Cassel had journeyed to Oregon for one of the first herds to reach Montana as well—though it had been Idaho then.

Bob Yoder—Robert's father—had turned from buffalo-hunting to cattle at about the same time, had made Horseshoe his own. A few other hardy souls, impressed by the example of these two, had followed suit. This was, comparatively, old settled country. Canyon, down below, where Bitter Creek joined the Musselshell, was quite a town.

Old memories, half-pleasant, half-mocking. The days when he and Robert Yoder had gone to school together in Canyon. That red-letter day when Anticlea McLean had first come to school, and the two of them had first come to blows over who should ride home with her. It had been Anticlea who had discovered that their ages and birthdays were the same, and had suggested a party.

Cassel shrugged impatiently. Water under the bridge was already far gone to the sea. He was conscious of a growing tightness as he rode. Plenty of cattle—but everyone that he had seen, though ranging here on Tincup, bore the Horseshoe on their right ribs. Not one sported the jaunty Tincup on their left shoulder.

'Beggar's brand,' he repeated tightly. 'Looks like it!'

Then he saw it—the old Tincup. On half a dozen cows. But it was blurred and blotched. A straight iron had been run through it as a vent. And as one of the cows turned, he saw the Horseshoe on her other side.

'So Yoder's lengthened his loop to include Tincup beef, has he?' Cassel muttered. 'He'd ought to know the vent's wrong, at least.'

But such a flagrant venting of an absent owner's brand, clapping his own on boldly, argued that Robert Yoder's arrogance had suffered no setback in the quartette of years. Cassel came around the bluff of a sprawling hill, and here was Tincup—the home ranch.

Sam Cassel had worked hard here, with big

visions of the future. Always it had been his gift to see that future as a splendid vista, unrolling in ever greater grandeur. He had been a big man, full-bearded, who looked and walked and talked like a prophet. And thought like one. A virtue which sometimes became a vice, since he had over-planned, had tried to compass into the space of a decade and a half what would take a life-time to do.

Tincup showed it. The twin lines of cottonwoods, set out along a half-mile of curving driveway leading up to the big log house, had never been quite completed. Some of them had lived and grown, were now attaining considerable size. But there were ugly gaps where many had died.

The house itself, huge and sprawling, lay lifeless under the late afternoon sun. Even the hazy peace of the day could not quite hide what the years had done to it. As he rode closer, Cassel saw that a door stood open, grass growing knee-high between it and the jamb, but recently grazed and trampled down. The milk-house, set above a spring, had been tipped over and left to lie, its stone foundation now a pile of rubble. The deep, clearly cold water of the spring beneath it had been slid and filled in by trampling cattle.

The bar sagged, unused. No one was here. He had expected that some of the crew would remain, looking after things. Old Dirk Hawes had given his word to keep things going, and Dirk's word was his bond. But it was apparent that Tincup had been abandoned and deserted for at least a year.

Cassel swung down from his horse, grim and cold. Each moment that letter which he had received was becoming clearer to him. He pushed through the open door of the house, and looked around with a cramping feeling at the pit of his stomach. This had been the big living room, or parlour. His father had planned it with a lot of pride, and in the window seat by the bay window, with its many small panes of multi-coloured glass—broken now—were rich, imported woods, oak and bird's-eye maple. Once the polish had been a thing to behold. It was still polished, where cattle had rubbed against it.

His mother had worked to make it her ideal of a home. In his boyish eyes, no more perfect place could be found.

Now it was a mockery. Cattle had crowded through the door during bad weather, huddling back in here for shelter. Their offal lay inches deep on the floor. They had pushed into other rooms, had even, it appeared, climbed the broad stairs venturesomely. Mountain rats, mice, other rodents, had moved in. The place was a stench, in the eyes as well as the nostrils.

Cassel's eyes grew darker. He turned and went out, and the little that had remained in him, warm and comfortable, had hardened to ice in that last hour. Without looking back, he climbed, a little awkwardly, into the saddle again. His face, long schooled to impassivity, since a man must hide his feelings when men died all around him or were torn to butchered meat, or else turn to gibbering insanity, was further cloaked by his beard now. But his eyes showed something of the deadly rage festering in him.

Yoder! This was his work. And for the thing he had done, desecrating a shrine, he merited death. But how could he mete out justice to the man, when that meant making Anticlea, only now a bride, so swiftly a widow as well?

The thought was double torment. Torment to discover that he loved her as deeply, as passionately, as at any time in the last five years—or the last ten, for that matter. She had known of this, of course, and had married the man who had done it. For that, she deserved no consideration. But that one spot of tenderness remained in him, and he knew that it would influence what he did, whether he liked it or not.

He was cold now, cold and deadly, as he came in sight of the buildings of Horseshoe, in the settling dusk of evening. Bob Yoder had not planned on so magnificent a scale as had his neighbour, but Horseshoe looked what it was—the hub of a big ranch, successful, busy, and comfortable enough. The barn outshone the house here, as on most ranches. There were evidences in plenty of it being lived in. Men clustered about the bunk house, horses rolled in the corrals, smoke arose from chimneys. It was all unchanged from four years ago, only busier.

Three men were coming in from the range. One, a big man with a placid, blank, baby-like face and cold grey eyes which belied the rest of him, and twin guns hanging loose in holsters. The man who rode beside him talked loudly, his tone jovial, but it was as though he masked a lean and ugly disposition thereby. Baby-Face addressed him as Brager.

The third man rode a little in advance of the other two, on a big sorrel stallion. Robert Yoder, little changed in four years. He was a blocky man, with a wide, smooth-shaven, almost handsome face, which made Cassel uncomfortably conscious of his own beard, reminded him that one day he must shave it off. Yoder's brown hair, which still curled a little, was beginning to thin in front, but not too much. Blue eyes that could turn as chill as steel were set a little too close together, but few people were apt to notice.

And he was tall—so much so that his blockiness hardly showed now, even in the saddle. He pulled up abruptly, a little startled, as Cassel reined in front of him, and for a moment there was blankness in his face, and then sudden recognition and with it apprehension in his eyes. Then that was gone, and his face was reserved and calculating. The two had pulled to a stop a little behind him.

'Why, hello, Cassel,' Yoder said, and lounged easily in the saddle. 'Didn't know you were back, yet.'

'I'm back,' Cassel said, and silence drifted between them for a long moment, the few, brief memories of comradeship, crowded out by the times when they had clashed and hated. It seemed now that there had never been anything else between them.

Yoder glanced toward the bunkhouse, and the men there within call, and nodded curtly to the other two.

'You and Baby-Face can go on in, Brager,' he said. 'Did you want to talk to me, Cassel?'

'I've just been to Tincup,' Cassel said tightly.

'I warned you, four years ago, of what would happen if you went off and left it,' Yoder said harshly, a little arrogant. 'It's no more than you had a right to expect.'

'Maybe not,' Cassel agreed. 'But the government called—and it happened to be my country.'

Yoder shrugged his big shoulders impatiently.

'What of it?' he demanded. 'I got my draft notice the same day. But I wasn't a fool.'

'No. You hired a substitute.'

'Poor men make better cannon fodder than rich, in the nature of things. You could have done the same. Tincup wasn't bankrupt—then.'

'What do you mean, then? I see you've been runnin' your cattle over my land, even putting your brand on my stock. But the land's still there—and there must be some stock left that you haven't butchered.'

Yoder looked at him in frank amazement.

'Your land?' he repeated. 'Your cattle? Haven't you heard? Tincup's mine, now. I don't brand cattle unless they belong to me.'

'How do you mean, Tincup's yours? How could it be?'

'The winter of '43 was a hard one. I managed to get through all right, by careful management and hard work. Most others didn't. Tincup was one. You'd left Dirk Hawes in charge. A good man—for punchin' cows. But no business sense. He lost nearly every head of stock, that winter. Borrowed from the Canyon bank and bought more, that spring. A man had just driven a bunch in from the east. Nice lookin' stock—' Yoder shrugged scornfully. 'Wanted to sell them to me. I wouldn't touch 'em. Knew they couldn't stand the winters here. They died, the next winter. Nineteen out of every twenty. But you must have heard.'

'I didn't get much mail—moving around,

fighting,' Cassel said tonelessly.

'But you must have heard of that.' Yoder looked a little concerned. 'I supposed of course you did. Even soldiers get mail.'

His face was a dim mask in the dusk now, but his voice had warmed a little. Cassel shook his head.

'I spent fourteen months in Andersonville,' he said. 'Maybe that accounts for it.'

'Jail, eh? Maybe so. Well, the bank was failing. I had to take it over to save the depositors. There was nothing left to do, to protect myself, but to take over Tincup, too. Hawes died that second winter, got pneumonia trying to save some of those cows. Tincup was gone, right then.'

'There's supposed to be a year of redemption, after a mortgage is foreclosed,' Cassel reminded.

'That year was up two months ago,' Yoder said tightly.

CHAPTER TWO

Cassel rode for town, a little dazed by what he had learned. Beggar's brand! Now it was true enough. No news of it had reached him. Whatever letters might have told of calamity had somehow failed to ever catch up with him. If he had known—but even if he had known, it could have made no difference. There was nothing that he could have done.

Yoder had warned him that he was a fool to go away and leave Tincup. And he had been right. By hiring a substitute to fight for him, paying out a few hundred dollars, Yoder had made thousands. Cassel, by going when his country called, had lost everything.

Yoder had not asked him in for the night, or even for supper. That was customary, on the range, but Cassel had understood, had been just as well satisfied. Anticlea was there, and he had no wish to meet her then, and under such conditions—and on top of all that he had learned to-day. Homecoming!

He had returned, but to no home. No welcome, such as a returning veteran might have expected. Now he knew there would be none. A few old acquaintances might feel sorry for him, but this country was Robert Yoder's country now. He, Clyde Cassel, former major in the Army of the United States, was just Cassel now, of Beggar's Brand—Tincup had been kicked over, spilled completely. Even his girl had thrown him over, had married the victor.

The magnitude of the disaster, and the completeness of it, was just now beginning to penetrate. A strong, ruthless man, utterly competent—that was what Anticlea had said of him. Now he'd need to be, to live at all.

Canyon was little changed as he rode into

it. A rather sleepy cow town, its only connection with the outside world the daily stages from east and west, or the slow-moving lines of freight wagons which groaned and creaked in with supplies now and again. So far as he could tell, it had suffered no outward change. There was the big pile of the Mercantile, right in the middle of town, yet set apart by itself. And the saloons, the livery stables, a few scattered houses.

He left his horse at one of the barns, turned towards the *Cattleman*. The two-storey, log hotel had never been much of a hostelry, but beggars, he reflected tightly, couldn't be choosers. He pushed open the door, stood in the lobby a minute, and sensed change here.

The big bar at one end of the lobby was gone. Instead of the crowd who usually loitered through until midnight, and kept the real customers of the hotel from anything but disturbed sleep, the room was virtually empty. Lace curtains covered the windows, comfortable chairs were set about, and the bar-section had been partitioned off into a new room, living quarters, apparently, for whoever ran the *Cattleman* now. Plainly, it had changed ownership in four years.

He saw her then, busily writing at a desk behind the counter. A straight-backed girl with soft brown hair loosely piled on her head, who looked up briefly, considered him, and went on with her writing. He pushed towards the counter, where an open register lay, flipped it around, and signed his name grimly. Clyde Cassel.

As he did so, someone entered from the new-made room. Another woman, with brown hair which was slowly greying, a tired, worried-looking face. But pleasant. He guessed instantly that these would be mother and daughter.

'Good evening,' she greeted pleasantly. 'Did you wish a room?' She glanced at the register, and then quickly at him. 'Mr. Cassel? You—you used to be—on Tincup?'

'Yes,' he agreed, sensing that here, for the first time since his return, was a show of friendliness.

'We've heard of you—though we're new here since your day. We'd like to welcome you back to Bitter Creek, at least.'

Bitter Creek, he thought, and reflected that it had been named better than he knew. But the woman was speaking again, her voice warm and somehow rich with friendliness.

'I'm Mrs. Kenney. This is my daughter, Kathleen. We want you to feel that you're home again—to make this your home just as long as you stay here.'

Kathleen had risen, turned. She was taller than he had thought, Cassel saw now, and her smile was warm as she held out her hand.

'Mother doesn't mean that quite the way she said it, Mr. Cassel,' she said. 'We do want you to feel at home as long as you stay here—but we aren't trying to drum up trade by asking you to stay and I—'

She checked suddenly, only now conscious of Cassel's empty sleeve, as he extended his left hand in turn.

'I hope you'll excuse me,' he said. 'I haven't much choice.'

'Oh, I—I'm sorry,' Kathleen blurted, and flushed painfully. 'I—I didn't know—though I knew, of course, that you were a veteran—'

'It's quite all right,' Cassel said. 'I've trained myself so that I can do almost as well with one arm as I once did with two.'

Mrs. Kenney's eyes were full of sympathy.

'I was just coming to call Kathleen to supper,' she said. 'But won't you join us? We'd love to have you.'

Cassel hesitated. Concern or sympathy irritated him. But he sensed the real friendliness here, their desire to welcome him home, to try and atone a little for what else he had found here. And he was hungry, while the smells wafting out were tantalizing.

'I'll be glad to,' he agreed.

★   ★   ★

Kathleen noted how skilful he had become in the use of one hand. There seemed to be few things which he could not do. And for the course of the meal it was as though he had deliberately put aside other things, had set out to make himself agreeable. He talked lightly but well. He was, as Mrs. Kenney expressed it later, a companionable man.

But Kathleen could see that this was only a mask. That when he looked at her, he did not really see her. She guessed that, if he saw any woman, he was seeing again the face of Anticlea, for once or twice she saw a shadow of pain deep in his eyes. It was there only for a moment, but clear enough.

She had no knowledge of the letter which he had received only that day. But it was common talk in the town that she had jilted Cassel in favour of Robert Yoder. And somehow, Kathleen sensed that he had not known of any of this until he returned here, that his hurt was new and raw. Part of it was more than guesswork with her, and built on certain knowledge.

For, only a few days before, Anticlea had been in the *Cattleman*, along with a couple of friends. The three of them had talked with a careless disregard for who might overhear them, and Anticlea had said enough that Kathleen understood. One phrase came vividly to her mind now.

'It's not as though he had been hurt, or anything, in the war,' Anticlea had exclaimed. 'If he'd even been wounded, he might have some claim on me. But he's gone through four years—seeing other women, I suppose, those Southern beauties, forgetting all about me. Why, the letters I've had, you could almost count on my fingers! And coming out a Major! It's just been one long holiday for him!'

Maybe that was what Anticlea believed. Probably it was what she was anxious to make herself believe, now that she had broken her promise to Cassel, Kathleen had thought at the time. Now, learning of the long, bitter months which he had spent in prison—though he had said little about them—seeing his empty sleeve, she knew how vain and petty had been Anticlea's excuses. And thought how shallow they would sound, even in Anticlea's own pretty ears, when she learned the truth which she might have discovered by waiting only a little longer.

But she hadn't wanted to wait—not for his return. Cassel knew that now. Seeing him, face to face, it might not be so easy to say those specious excuses. She had long since made up her mind to marry Robert Yoder, and now the thing was done.

The food was tasteless in his mouth, though he knew that it was good. He excused himself, and returned to the livery barn for his turkey. It was a light enough bag of duffel to pack easily, with one hand. He had acquired little enough, in four years. Experience was about all. And that could be packed in the compass of a man's brain.

Tramping back, through the soft dusk, he climbed the stairs to his room, and noted that it was better than rooms at the *Cattleman* had been in the old days. There were lacy curtains at the windows, and a new, potted geranium with a blood-red blossom on his stand. That latter, he guessed, was a special addition since supper time. On the floor was a braided rag rug, its bright colours adding a touch of cheer to the drab walls. The room was cleaner than in the old days, too.

He sensed the kindness in the Kenneys, mother and daughter, then shook his head impatiently. Once the Cassels had been great in the valley of the Bitter. It was conceivable that he, a Major just returned from the wars, might still have a little money, sufficient to pay for a room for a while. This was just good business, to favour one who might be a good customer, when customers were scarce. His mouth twisted bitterly.

That would be it, of course. He had seen enough, learned enough at heavy cost, to know that it could not be anything else. If Anticlea would do this to him, who was any better? There would be two verities—life and death. No more.

Impatience stirred in him. He had been tired, a little while before, from the long trail, his thoughts rather expectantly on bed and a long, long sleep. Now he knew that he couldn't sleep. He craved action, anything to keep him from thinking—or at least to force his riot of thoughts to the recesses of his mind.

He went out, hesitated, and crossed the street to the *Northern Bar*. It might be a good idea to get drunk. But even as he stepped inside, the stale odours of liquor and tobacco, and the heavy accumulated reek of unwashed bodies met his nostrils, he knew that he had no desire for liquor—or for anything else here.

Yet he went on in, chiefly because there was nowhere else to go. A few men greeted him in mild surprise, but all with an innate caution behind their words. He slid into a chair where a poker game was in progress, and saw their wordless question as they looked at his empty sleeve. His bearded, immobile face betrayed nothing.

'I can't deal, gentlemen,' he said. 'But I trust that the rest of you will share my turn. Otherwise I think you'll find me able to hold up my own end.'

He displayed an adroitness which astonished them. Flipping up each card in turn for an instant, laying it face down in a neat pile. Without looking at them a second time, his fingers riffled across them briefly, sorting, sliding them into new positions. That alone told them that here was a poker player—for those who had not known him of old. A clear, precise mind that could note a fact and catalogue it and keep it ready for exact use when needed. He picked the cards up then, held them spread fan-wise with accustomed ease, and when it came his turn to play, flipped one loose with a motion of his little finger. Always it landed right side up and in place.

For the first hour, men gathered at the table to watch the show, for here was something new and different. With his skill an accepted thing, interest shifted to the game itself. Two of the players he had known of old. Mike O'Brien was a cowboy, a genial man with upturned eyebrows which served to give him a perpetually surprised look. Blue Chip was a gambler by profession, a tall, clean-shaven, emotionless man who had never given any other name, but who was known as a square gambler.

The other man, who was addressed as Judd, had taken a hand after another player had stepped out, declaring that the stakes were getting a little high for him. Without asking permission, Judd had slid into the vacated chair, dropped a couple of gold coins on the table in exchange for chips, and so cut himself in.

Within a few minutes, Cassel had him catalogued. The man was silent enough as he played, yet when he spoke there was a bluster and swagger behind his words, just as behind the way he slapped his cards down, or reached hungrily to rake in a pot. Big, almost beefy, he had a yellow moustache and eyes to match. He packed a gun in open holster, and hitched it around ostentatiously whenever he shifted his position.

It was plain to Cassel that Blue Chip did not like the man, though he said nothing. And that O'Brien was uneasy, his good humour drying up at the source with a startling abruptness. Probably the two were a little afraid of Judd, he decided. And wondered at that, for neither man was lacking in courage.

Cassel had entered the game with no thought of winning. Merely because he needed the outlet, a chance to be doing something which would help to tire him so that finally he could sleep, would occupy his mind awhile. But, as though having struck him down hard enough during the day, and now in a mood to relent, Lady Luck was smiling on him. Almost without exception he drew good cards.

By midnight, he saw that, with a little more luck, he might come out of this game with a small stake. He had entered it with the remains of his salary from the army in his pocket—less than fifty dollars, which, he had discovered that afternoon, was all that the owner of a beggar's brand could lay claim to in the world. And he knew already, that most men would not care to hire a cowboy with only one arm.

A few men turned as a newcomer entered the saloon and paused at the table. Even Judd looked up with a grudging respect in his eyes. For this man was Paddy—and Paddy was Canyon.

At least, it had been that way four years ago. Paddy had come to Canyon, walking in on hob-nailed boots where only the nails had held the leather together to keep his feet off the ground. A genial, smiling man, with the quickest eyes that Cassel had ever seen—and the smile never got as deep as those eyes. Behind them, Cassel had long since discovered, there was often no geniality at all. The cold, poker face of Blue Chip was warm compared to the coldness that could lurk behind this man's false friendliness.

But it was that quality of cold alertness which had found its proper field for expansion, here in Canyon. Two days after his coming, a man whose name had long since been forgotten, had acquired a partner in the *Northern Bar*. Paddy had paid with fear, Cassel guessed—a deliberate announcement that he was taking himself a half-interest.

Certain it was that there had been fear in the other man's face for the next few days during which he had lingered. Then he had disappeared between two days, nobody knew where, or how, or was much disposed to ask. Few had cared for the man in any case, or what happened to him. And few, probing behind that encompassing front of geniality, cared to question Paddy, then or later, as to how he did things.

But it was sufficiently in evidence that he did them. He had been owner then of the *Northern*. A year later, he was boss of the town. His word, seldom given openly, was law—such as Canyon knew. And from the way these men looked at him now, Cassel judged that the *status quo* was unchanged.

Which was some matter for wonder. For, four years ago, Robert Yoder declared, quite openly, that the Bitter Creek country wasn't big enough to hold both Paddy and himself. Since then, Yoder had flourished and expanded like tumbleweed on the prairie. Yet here was Paddy, big and genial as ever, at his shoulder now.

Paddy dropped one hand familiarly on Cassel's right shoulder, held it there a moment. His face was beaming.

''Tis a pleasure to see ye back in Canyon, Clyde me b'y,' he said. 'The country has been the worse for your absence, and is the better for your return.'

'Is it, Paddy?' Cassel asked, and flicked a card on to the pile. Paddy's words, he knew, meant little. But the more genial the smile and the tone, the more should any man walk with caution. And Paddy was very genial tonight.

Yet it could mean the opposite. In four years, since they both flourished, Paddy and Yoder could have made their peace and entered into an alliance. But if they had failed to do so—then Paddy's warm welcome might mean something else.

'Sure that it is,' Paddy said vigorously. He lifted his hand, held it almost as if giving a benediction. His hair, Cassel saw, was as long as ever, but it had greyed considerably in those four years. When he smiled that way, Paddy had the look of a parson, rather than what he was.

''Tis hopin' I am that ye'll foind toime to come to me office soon, where we can have a foine visit, for old toimes sake,' Paddy went on. 'Be seein' ye, Clyde me b'y.'

He nodded, drifted on and out again. He had heard of this game, of course, had gone out of his way to come here and deliver this summons—for it amounted to little less. Why? At least, it would do no harm, in a day or so, to find out.

His mind on Paddy, Cassel was a little startled when Judd flung down his cards impatiently.

'Your luck's too damned good for honest men!' he growled. 'Far too good, without a break! Sojer's tricks! I've seen 'em before!'

Deliberately, he reached out, and swept the winnings, which belonged to Cassel, across the table, started to stuff them into his own pocket. A thousand dollars. Cassel came to his feet. 'That's my money,' he said, and his voice would have warned most men.

'It would be, if you'd played a straight game,' Judd mocked. 'But as it is—no. And what do you intend to do about it?'

Cassel looked at him a moment.

'I'll show you,' he said. And turned on his heel and left the room. As he went out, he heard the mocking gust of laughter which bellowed up from Judd's mighty chest, following him out the door.

CHAPTER THREE

Cassel's lips were set in a thin tight line as he walked across the street. The *Cattleman* was dark now, for the night was well worn. Every other place in town, in fact, save the *Northern*, had long since closed. Only the game had kept it open.

He let himself in, climbed the stairs to his room, remembering to tread as lightly as possible on the stairs. His mood was harsh and ugly, and as a boy, it would have been his impulse to slam doors and tramp resoundingly. Now he walked lightly, and to those who knew him, that would have been hailed a dangerous sign. Anticlea had said that he was a strong man, and ruthless.

Rummaging in his turkey, he found his revolver, drew it out and examined it briefly. It had not seemed necessary to him to wear a gun, that evening. A one-armed man was perhaps better without one. But he had taken Judd's measure too accurately to doubt the need now. He slid it into the band of his belt, went back and across the street.

As he had counted on, Judd was still there, downing a drink at the bar, bragging to the others who remained of how he had curried a cheat. Lost in his own admiration, he did not hear Cassel until the others started to sidle back and away. Warned then, he swung suddenly, setting his half-emptied glass on the bar so hard that the glass cracked and the whisky began to seep out, to spread in a little pool, unnoticed, almost like blood.

Cassel's face, where the beard did not hide it, was white now. His voice rapped hard and sure.

'I'll take what belongs to me now, Judd. Lay it on the bar!'

Judd stared, taking a step backward. His face flushed, then paled. He half-dropped a hand towards his own gun, then checked the motion. Cassel's voice was mocking, biting.

'Go on and draw, if that's what you want,' he said. 'I've killed your kind before!'

Judd hesitated. The sureness, the bluster, had gone out of him. He was, Cassel judged, a man with courage enough to match the looseness of his mouth, on ordinary occasions. But this was something he had not counted on. There were times when a man could feel death, could taste it, smell it, like an odour—when it prickled the senses and put its weight upon you. Cassel had felt it that way, more than once. He saw that, and probably for the first time in his life, it had dented the hard crust of Judd's consciousness, that he was feeling it now.

Judd ran a thick tongue over suddenly dry lips. He was staring at Cassel as if hypnotized. A second time he tried to drive his hand downward, and found it palsied. He nodded jerkily.

'Sure, feller,' he said thickly. 'I—I was just sort of hoorawin' you a little—tryin' to see what was behind that set of whiskers. You got what it takes, all right. I never aimed to keep the money.'

He delved in a pocket now and brought it out, so hastily that some of it spilled. He piled it on the bar, and Cassel watched without speaking. Judd tried again.

'You sure are all I ever heard about you,' he went on. 'And that bein' so, we're mighty glad to welcome yuh back to Canyon—'

Contemptuously, Cassel swept up the money, stuffed it into his own pocket. He had not made even one threatening gesture towards his own gun, plain to see there in his belt. Now, saying nothing, not even looking at Judd, he walked to the door and out.

He was not aware, as he climbed the stairs to his room again, that Kathleen Kenney watched from behind a door open a small crack. That she had seen him come in before, had sensed the teneseness in him, and found it partly understandable. She had heard, earlier in the evening, of the game which was in progress over at the *Northern*, and of the man he was playing against.

Three minutes, she had seen him go out again, and where the moonlight crept in at the window and lay across the lobby, she had seen its glint on the naked gun he carried, and knew why he had returned.

She had stood there then, in bare feet, shivering a little, though not with the cold, listening, tense and strained—just why, she did not quite know. What difference did it make to her, after all? Plenty of men had died in Canyon—sudden, violent death was almost a daily occurrence. And this man, even though he was a returned soldier, a man who had lost an arm, and a man who had been given a dirty deal—still, he was only one more roomer in the hotel, a stranger to her, no more to her than any one of the endless procession who came and went.

Yet she had stood and strained her ears, and shivered in a nameless apprehension, waiting for the shot which did not come. Now, as she saw him re-enter the lobby and climb again to his room, the gun still in place, she expelled her breath in a long, shivering sigh. What she had feared had not happened, and for that she was curiously glad, even as she was at a loss to understand. For he must have clashed with the man Judd, who was Robert Yoder's foreman at Horseshoe. There could be no other reason for getting the gun.

His return, and the lack of any shooting, was puzzling. For Judd had killed more than one man, there across the street.

Cassel slept late the next morning. It was satisfying to sleep, as he had dreamed of doing so many times. A dreamless sleep in a good bed, with security around you. He awoke refreshed, a little surprised. Somehow that last episode had relaxed him, washed his mind temporarily of the other things which bothered.

Not until he had washed and dressed did he bother to count the money which he had won the evening before. There was, he found, more than he had expected—nearly twelve hundred dollars. And approximately a thousand of that was out of Judd's pocket. The foreman of Horseshoe had not had so much with him, but had used his credit, borrowing from the house. The result, to Cassel, was gratifying. At least, he wouldn't be an actual beggar—not for a while.

He combed his hair and beard and descended to the lobby, intending to go quietly out. It was too late for breakfast anywhere of course; too early for dinner. But that didn't worry him. He had missed plenty of meals in the past few years, had learned to eat when and where he could.

The odour of fresh frying eggs and crisping bacon, of steaming coffee came to his nostrils, then Kathleen was greeting him smilingly, beckoning him to come to the little kitchen where he had eaten the evening before.

'Mother's frying eggs and bacon for you,' she said. 'You'll be hungry, of course.'

They had, of course, heard him stirring above stairs. Cassel felt a little surprised and bewildered by this kindness. For it was nothing less, nor more. They knew that he had nothing—he was not owner of a big ranch, nor any figure of romance—not with that empty sleeve.

'You shouldn't have bothered,' he protested, as he allowed them to lead him to a seat. There was a big stack of hot cakes and honey as well, he saw, and the coffee was as he liked it—strong and black.

'It was no trouble,' Mrs. Kenny assured him. 'I like a cup of coffee myself at this time of day.' She smiled serenely at him, stirring her own cup, and Kathleen was taking a cup as well, seated across the table from him—and doing it, he guessed, just to make him feel at home.

'It's really in the nature of a premium for

what you did last night,' Kathleen said, and her smile was slow, grave. 'It's all over town this morning—how you made Judd back down. That deserves recognition. No one else has ever done it.'

'It was a brave thing to do,' Mrs. Kenney said. 'But you look like a man who can take care of himself.'

'I've had a lot of it to do,' Cassel said, a little shortly.

'Which is lucky,' she nodded. 'For did you, or did you not, know that Judd is foreman at Horseshoe?'

They saw, from his eyes, that he had not known. But he drank his coffee without any other change of expression, considering what he had learned. It did make a difference, beyond question. He had known for sure the day before how Robert Yoder stood about his return to Bitter Creek, had sensed the old hate rising up like a fetid breath above a sink-hole. That hate stemmed from far back, but there had been the shadow of old friendship partially balancing it in the old days.

That was long gone. Yoder had wronged him during the years of his absence, wronged him doubly, grievously. That was enough to make any man hate, Cassel knew—the more bitterly, because of his own sense of guilt.

It had been clear, there in the dusk of the day before. And with Judd as foreman of

Horseshoe, and the story all over Bitter Creek of how he had been faced down, humiliated by a one-armed man—

'I didn't know it,' Cassel said, and his moustache lifted in the first smile his face had known in weeks, as he set his cup down. 'That's mighty good coffee, Mrs. Kenney. Could I have another cup? His being foreman of Horseshoe—that makes it interesting.'

It did. Life, the evening before, seemed to have reached a cross-roads. To have come to a stopping-place. Almost to an end. But this morning there was promise. They'd try to run him out of Bitter Creek, to kill him. He knew that it was as inevitable now as for powder to burn once the spark had reached it. And he suddenly knew that he was going to stay here, that in the battle which impended there would be a new interest in life.

What he would do, beyond staying, he didn't know. He had no plans, but there was no great hurry for any. He remembered Paddy, and turned to where Paddy had his office. No longer in the *Northern*, but in the rear of the Bitter Creek General Mercantile Store. A tremendous building, which handled everything anyone wanted to buy, with the exception of liquor, found in Paddy's half-dozen saloons.

On the street he encountered Blue Chip, jowls blue from the razor, blinking a little in the sunlight, as though unaccustomed to daylight at all. The gambler's face was as expressionless as ever to-day, but his eyes held warmth for a moment.

'I'm glad to see you alive this morning, Cassel,' he said.

'Thanks, Blue Chip, I'm finding myself glad to be alive—surprising as that may sound,' Cassel admitted.

'Because you're thinking of the fight you have on your hands,' Blue Chip agreed. 'You always loved a fight.'

'Did I?' Cassel considered this. 'Maybe you're right.'

'I know I am. That's why you went away to the wars, instead of staying to look after Tincup—or hiring a substitute.'

Cassel made a little gesture of disgust.

'I've seen too many substitutes,' he said. 'Men hired for four or five hundred dollars—to go through hell, and, the chances are, die for it. It's too cheap a price for dying. A man should do that for himself.'

'You aren't so much changed, are you? But Yoder had other ideas.'

'So he did. And they seem to have paid him well.'

'Very well. He got a bargain, when he hired his substitute—always supposing that, had he been wearing the same shoes, he'd have gotten the same bullet through his heart.'

'The man was killed, then?'

'Yes. He was Tom Kenney.'

Cassel turned, jarred a little by the name, and the gambler's tone of voice.

'Kenney?' he repeated. 'You mean—?'

'Mrs. Kenney's son. Kathleen's brother. That's why they're here. Yoder had never paid the money. They came—Tom was still alive then, to collect it for him. Yoder had gotten hold of the *Cattleman*. He turned that over to them to try and make it square—and to try and make an impression on Kathleen, I think.'

'Did he succeed?'

'He wouldn't have, with her, even if the news of Tom hadn't come within the week. Kathleen's not for sale.'

The news disgusted Cassel, though not particularly surprising him. Anticlea had married Robert Yoder—yet she must have known of his affairs with other women. They had been no secret in this town. And marriage would not change him. Well, she had gotten what she wanted.

And Kathleen—Mrs. Kenney—he was beginning to understand a little better now. In a way, they were probably welcoming him home in place of Tom—since he had disdained to hire a substitute, had fought and all but died, had left a piece of himself on some forgotten field of battle.

'You'll want to know the set-up in this town, now,' Blue Chip was speaking again.

'You're heading to see Paddy, I presume?'

'Why, yes, I thought I'd look in on him.'

'I don't know just what his game is,' Blue Chip said guardedly. 'Few do. Yoder set out to run him out of the country. They were both getting too big for competition. Of late there's been a truce. My opinion is, they're partners now.'

'Thanks,' Cassel said, as the gambler went on. That was well to know, with such a conference coming up. He entered the Mercantile, went the length of the big room, and climbed the stairs to the balcony across the rear. A man lounged near the foot of the stairway, another was at the top. Gun-guards. Both of them looked casually at him, but gave him no more than a second glance. Plainly, he was expected.

Paddy opened the door before he could reach it, dragged him warmly inside. To-day, he looked more like a benevolent preacher than ever, and it was almost as a shock when he pushed a box of cigars towards his visitor and struck a match for him.

"Tis good to see ye back, Clyde, me b'y,' he said. 'And while I was anxious for a worrd wid ye last avenin', afther what ye did to top it off—that makes it all the better.'

The room was changed with the years. There was a rich, imported rug on the floor, a costly desk, oil paintings on the walls. Cassel surveyed it and nodded.

'Judd, you mean?'

'Himself.' Paddy was not one to waste words when there was no point to it. 'He has six notches on his gun. 'Tis a wee bit surprised I am that ye faced him down—though to be sure, ye have a way with ye.'

'I'd have killed him, and he knew it,' Cassel said shortly.

'I believe all of that.' Paddy surveyed him anew. 'Ye always was a harrd man, Clyde. 'Tis no matter of surprise that ye became a major.'

Cassel waited, smoking. Paddy grinned.

'With Tincup gone, and Horseshoe—includin' Judd—wantin' to run ye out or kill ye, ye'll be open for a good job av the right sort, maybe?'

'I might be,' Cassel conceded cautiously.

'So I thought. I've been needin' a man could fill the job—and findin' him hard to foind till now. And ye'll be needin' the job to fill your hand for what's ahead. Say the word, and startin' now ye're Marshal of Bitter Creek.'

CHAPTER FOUR

Even though he was a poker player, Cassel's surprise showed in his eyes. Whatever he had expected, this wasn't it. He probed for Paddy's reason, and found it hard to find.

'For what reason?' he asked bluntly, and Paddy grinned again.

'For this and that,' he said. 'Such as havin' a bit of law in town for a change. Do ye take the job, Clyde, there'll be no strings attached. We've a committee here in Canyon. They delegated me to foind a man would fill the shoes av a marshal, and then to pin a badge on him. The pay is good. The job is a tough one—for most men. For yoursilf, it shouldn't be too harrd.'

No strings attached! That was a sweeping promise, coming from Paddy. But there would still be a reason behind it. Paddy was making no secret of the trouble between himself and Robert Yoder. As marshal, his authority would extend beyond Canyon, would pretty well take in the Bitter Creek country. And that would inevitably, sooner or later—and sooner rather than later—bring him into conflict with Horseshoe.

Was that what Paddy wanted? Had he come to a parting of the ways with Yoder? Or was this a gesture on his part to show his own authority? There was no telling, but Cassel made up his mind.

'Pin on your star,' he said. 'I'll wear it.'

''Tis the sort of answer I thought ye'd give,' Paddy nodded approvingly, and taking a badge from the top drawer of his desk, proceeded to pin it on Cassel's coat. 'If ye feel the need av a deputy, say but the word, and pick your man.'

That was fair enough. Cassel stood up, went out, and was conscious of the sudden startled scrutiny of the gun-guards as their attention was caught by the badge he wore.

Some things were beginning to fit into place. It had been no chance happening, Judd sitting in that game the night before. Judd had known who he was, and had chosen that method to humiliate him, or, if he showed resentment, to kill him. The thing was plain enough now. Men did not go out of their way to do such things to strangers.

Only it hadn't worked out quite as Judd had planned. He had been the one to be humiliated, and being a killer by reputation, that was something he would never forgive.

★ ★ ★

Resentment rode with Judd as he returned to Horseshoe. It was a two-hour ride out from town, with a good horse, and he rode no other kind. Fury boiled in him like warmed-over coffee grounds re-cooked to get the last dregs, a dark and bitter brew. The fact that the whole thing had been his own fault, that he had allowed himself to be faced down by a one-armed man, and that the story would be all over the country before another night, increased the hate in him.

A harvest moon rode the sky trails to-night, the air, even at this hour, was soft and balmy. The scent of ripening earth was a tangy fragrance like that of a well-filled granary. A coyote watched him pass, not even moving to one side, fat and sleek with contentment. Cattle, bedded down near the road, stirred and resettled themselves for more sleep.

That was half the trouble. Judd was a man who liked his sleep. And to-night he was being cheated of most of it. He'd get a couple of hours, no more. And to-morrow—

But his mind was working again now, the rage driven out, replaced by a cool calculation. Robert Yoder was sure to hear the full tale of this. It would be better if it came from him, and first.

So it was that the crew of Horseshoe, abroad at the usual hour, looked with mild surprise to see Judd stirring among the first. At such a time, after getting in late, he usually claimed the prerogative of a foreman and slept an extra hour or so. But to-day he was headed up towards the big house while the dew still caught the early sun. He saw Yoder, always an early riser, and, beyond him, at the house, Anticlea, and paused for a moment to fill his eyes with her beauty. It was as though all the glory of early sunrise had gathered in a halo round her head, for her hair was the colour of the sun, a bright, vivid colour to match her cheeks and the sparkle in her eyes. She, too, was up early this morning—more so than usual. He caught his employer's eye on him, and withdrew behind a corral.

'How'd it go?' Yoder asked without preamble.

Judd grinned faintly. It cost him something to achieve that grin, but he never blustered with Yoder, and in it he put just the right shade of contempt and self-disparagement.

'Not so good,' he said. 'He made a fool of me.'

'How come?'

'He'd been lucky at poker,' Judd explained, and at the interest in Yoder's eyes, gave details. 'The way he can handle cards with one hand, is somethin' to see.'

'He always was a poker player,' Yoder said matter-of-factly.

'Well, I aimed to prod him a little. Made out mebby I'd keep my money. Just ribbin' him.' He shook his head. 'That hombre's proddy as if he'd perched on a cactus. Threw a gun on me quicker'n scat!'

'So you paid up?'

'I paid up. And now everybody's laughin' at me.' Judd's shoulders hunched. 'I always like the last laugh.'

Yoder nodded, thoughtfully.

'Gives you a good excuse,' he said. 'For what you need to do. Listen: Mrs. Yoder wants to go in to town first thing this morning. She's heard that he's back. If she guessed that he was here, last evenin'—' he shrugged briefly.

'She insists on drivin' the bays. I can't go along, not this morning. So you go with her. Those cayuses are too high-strung for her to handle alone. Don't tangle with Cassel when she's around. But when you get the chance—give him warnin'.'

'I'll tend to it,' Judd agreed. The bays were a pretty pair of buggy horses, perfectly matched, tireless on the road. But with an incurable habit of running away at unexpected moments. Judd had no objections to riding to town with Anticlea Yoder. Indeed, the opportunity gave him pleasure which he was careful to dissemble from Yoder's eyes. But he knew the real reason why Robert Yoder was staying away, and it dampened his own pleasure as well. Yoder didn't want to meet Cassel again, not while Anticlea was seeing him for the first time as well.

Presently they were on the road, Anticlea driving, giving the bays their heads. Few horses could run too fast to suit her, or ever had been able to. She let them run, with a sort of breathless excitement in her eyes which was her greatest fascination, and Judd could see that there was an added sparkle to her to-day which had not been present for a long time.

He pondered that, a little puzzled. He was new to Bitter Creek since Cassel had left the country, but he had heard a lot about Cassel and Anticlea and Robert Yoder. It had seemed to him that Anticlea had made her decision to marry the man she really loved, urged thereto, perhaps, by the fact that he was a big man in this country now.

But to-day he wondered. Anticlea had been engaged to this Cassel—now she was anxious to see him again. Maybe Yoder knew what he was doing. The sooner Cassel was run out of Bitter Creek, the better it would be.

They reached town, bright with sunlight, shabby under its glare now that the dawn dew had lifted with its faint glamorous haze. The streets were heavy with dust, which eddied to every stroke of a horse's hoof, curled up in little eddies from the steel-shod buggy wheels. A gust of wind danced it in a little whirl, swinging it about them as if in mockery, choking, gritty. The horses tried to run, and were curbed with an impatient hand. Then the gust passed, Anticlea thrust the reins into Judd's hand and dabbed at her face with a wisp of handkerchief.

'Pah!' she exclaimed. 'Now I look a fright. Let me off here at the *Cattleman*, Judd. And take the team around to the livery stable.'

She climbed expertly down as he cramped the wheels, still rubbing impatiently at the dust, went inside the hotel. Few people were abroad on the street this early. The big Mercantile had one long wagon tied in front, and loomed like a misplaced giant among the smaller buildings which made up the town, set apart from all others as it was.

Judd came to the livery barn, and Big Tom came out to help him unhitch. Big Tom was a ponderous man, six feet and two inches in height, yet not looking tall because of the sheer bigness of him. In that, he was strongly like Yoder. He moved slowly for the most part, yet Judd was not deceived. He had seen him bend a steel bar to a letter U between his two hands; straighten it again as effortlessly. And he had seen him jump and grab the bridle of a rearing, kicking horse, moving with a speed which most men could never equal.

He turned the team over to Big Tom, and hesitated between two courses: whether to go to a saloon and kill time, or stretch out on the hay in the loft for some of the sleep he had missed the night before. But the day would be long and his eyes were heavy. He climbed and slept, and came down later, to see a faintly sardonic amusement in Big Tom's face.

'Sounds like you sawed a lot of wood, up there, Judd,' he said mildly. 'And you were so early abroad this mornin', looks like you must not 've even gone to bed, last night.'

'I had a good sleep—this time,' Judd assured him. 'And curry these cayuses good, will you? They need it.'

'Sure,' Big Tom agreed. 'Speakin' of curryin'—I hear that this Cassel curried you last night—kind of rough?'

'He caught me by surprise,' Judd growled. 'I wasn't lookin' for any trouble from a cripple. And what can you do against one, anyhow?'

'Yeah, that's the question. What? For I figger you'll aim to.'

'You're damn right I aim to,' Judd agreed. 'If he wants to act that way, he'll have to accept the responsibility. There's nothing left for him in this country, so he'll have to keep travellin'.'

'And you come to town to tell him so?'

'I sure did—'

Judd halted suddenly. He became aware that a third man had entered the shadowy stable, was standing just behind him. A prickling sensation like cold sweat chilled him, and he turned, saw Cassel fingering his beard with a look in his eyes even more chill.

'You were talkin' about me, Judd?' he asked.

He saw the shock come into Judd's eyes as they fastened on the law badge which he wore. And behind the shock was surprise that this thing could be so. For the moment, faced with the unknown, Judd was completely speechless.

'I like Bitter Creek,' Cassel said. 'It's been my country a long time, Judd—and I aim to stay.' He turned then, sauntered back out into the sunlight. Not hurrying. But the sun seemed to gather in that law badge and reflect back with a brightness out of all proportion to what it would have meant to any other man.

Judd stared, and knew that, despite the orders he had been given, he must consult Yoder before any further move. There was uneasiness in his eyes, and a resurgence of hate which lent a bitter sparkle of anticipation.

★   ★   ★

Anticlea, struggling with an excitement such as she had not felt for years, was a little surprised at herself. Not much given to introspection, she wondered uneasily at her own feelings now. It was a natural thing to come to town, and if she should encounter Clyde Cassel in town, why, they had always been friends—

She had assured herself of that, even as she dressed for the trip to town. It was natural to see him again, now that he was back. She had written that note to him, breaking off their engagement, four months ago, the day before she had married Robert Yoder. She supposed that Cassel had received it months ago as well. The fact that he had come on here to Bitter Creek at long last might mean much or little.

It might mean trouble, she admitted frankly—trouble for Horseshoe, for her husband. For Cassel was, as she had said, a strong and ruthless man on occasion, and he might not take kindly to what had happened. She wanted to see him, for old friendship's sake, to prevent, if she could, any rupture now.

That was the reason which she had given to herself. But she knew now that it didn't quite fill the bill—any more than marriage to Robert Yoder had filled the bill. Up to this morning, she had never admitted, even to herself, that she was disappointed with the choice she had made. Yet, thinking of Cassel, knowing that, after four long years, he was back in Bitter Creek, that she might see him at any moment, gave her such a sense of excitement, of breathless expectancy, as she had not experienced since the day when she had agreed to marry him.

She hurried to the room which was kept for her at all times, here at the *Cattleman*, so that, on any trip to town, she might rest and refresh herself. Yoder had suggested a town house for that purpose, but she had preferred a room here. It had seemed to her that her husband had not been too pleased with the idea, but he had accepted it.

Now, having sponged her face and neck, removing the grime of the trip and cooling down a bit of the hot colour of excitement, she crossed to the Mercantile for the ostensible purpose of the visit—to do a bit of shopping. Later she had a bite to eat, and, not too satisfied, returned to the *Cattleman*. She had seen no sign of Cassel, and already she was impatient, but it was too early to start back for Horseshoe.

She paused in the lobby, enjoying the coolness of the big room. Red geraniums bloomed in the window, and to Anticlea's mind, the *Cattleman* was vastly improved from its old estate.

Kathleen Kenney was ironing, in a far corner of the room, having moved her board out into the lobby for the added coolness. She returned from the kitchen stove, carrying a heavy iron, pausing to test its heat with finger in mouth and touched to the iron for just a fleeting moment, and she looked across to Anticlea in her smart, trim outfit, noted that she was wearing a hat just purchased, and felt again the vague resentment that she had known before. This girl had everything—always she had had it, without any least effort on her part.

It was not that which bothered Kathleen. Some had and some did not. That was the way of the world. Her resentment was rooted in the fact that Anticlea had no least appreciation for what had been so lavishly bestowed upon her. And, to-day, in the thought that she would so coolly and callously toss aside a man like Cassel, with no thought of how she might hurt him in the process.

'My, it's cool and nice in here,' Anticlea said. 'And you look so comfortable, Kathleen.' She was not aware that her voice was patronising. 'Just as though you were made for such a job.' She leaned on the desk, and glanced idly down at the register, and her eyes widened suddenly at the bold signature there. She looked up, eyes still wide.

'Clyde Cassel,' she repeated. 'Is—is he here?'

'Right behind you,' Kathleen said, a little sharply, and, though her iron was still hot, moved almost angrily back into the kitchen.

CHAPTER FIVE

Cassel had just come in. He had gotten a brief satisfaction out of his encounter with Judd, and the surprised bewilderment in the foreman's eyes at sight of his marshal's badge. Clearly, what Paddy had done was the last thing that Judd had expected.

He was still considering that angle of it when he entered the lobby, and Anticlea turned and saw him.

He had not been thinking of her; nor expecting to find her in town. Not to-day. Horseshoe seemed at the moment a long way off.

Anticlea, he saw, had not changed much. That vivid freshness and excitement still abounded in her, the added sparkle and colour in her eyes and cheeks made her seem just as he had remembered her. She had matured a little more, yet she showed no real signs of four years of such change as he had known. If anything, she was more beautiful.

Her own surprise was equal to his. But something like dismay came into her eyes as she looked at him. He had been smooth-shaven when he went away, and now the long, full, black beard lent him a dignity, an austerity, a sense of strength and maturity which he had never possessed before.

In his face, where it was exposed, there was change as well—more particularly in his eyes. Here was one who had ridden away almost as a boy, filled with a boy's eager enthusiasm, bridged across all regrets of what the parting cost him. But he had returned a man. The enthusiasm, like the boyishness, had been burned away. His face was lined, his eyes had looked on life, and death, and unchancy things. She could see it all, the suffering that he had endured, the mark of the years of campaigning. And in that moment, for the first time, she saw his empty sleeve, and it shocked her like a blow in the face.

'Oh, Clyde,' she said, and the shock was in her voice. She moved towards him, her hand half-reached to touch his sleeve and fell back again. 'I didn't know—'

He saw in her face and her voice that she was telling the truth. She hadn't known. Nor, he knew then, had she even been able to guess. She had seen him ride away, a boy in her eyes. Somehow she had expected the same boy to return. Bitter Creek might be changed, Horseshoe swollen, Tincup swept away. But that there might be change in him had never entered her head.

'It's long past now,' he said, and harshness stirred in his tones. A man could suffer or die, and with her head in the clouds, she couldn't even imagine what might happen to him.

Yet that was unjust judgment, he knew in the same moment, as he saw the quick hurt in her eyes, the tremble of her lips before she stilled them. She was more beautiful than ever—and she was Anticlea.

'I'm sorry,' she said. 'Terribly sorry, Clyde. And—the way I've treated you—what must you think of me?'

He looked at her, and she saw in his eyes what he would not put into words. He had never been a man for pretty speeches. Nor one to say what he didn't mean. War had not schooled him in such arts and graces. He had no desire, in that moment, to hurt her. So he would not tell her of how she had hurt him, or that he considered her selfish and ungrateful and grasping. But she could see it in his face.

'I wish—I could die!' she gasped, and the words, totally unexpected even by herself, came with stark honesty. She turned, flushing scarlet, stumbled across to the door and out. She found herself in the full sunshine, walking fast, before her mind started to function again. Nothing was as she had anticipated it, nothing as she had planned—and worse, nothing was as she had believed it to be.

She was nearly to the livery barn, she saw, and she turned in, calling imperatively to Big Tom to hitch up the team for her at once. Big Tom, moving stolidly around the end of a stall, a pitchfork of hay held lightly in one hand, reached with the other to remove a straw from between his teeth, minded to protest. He knew that Robert Yoder did not want her to take those untrustworthy bays out alone, and that Judd, in black and bitter mood, had moved off down town and was now in some saloon.

But the protest died unspoken as he saw her face. No man had ever accused Big Tom of any lack in courage, but he was a man who knew his limitations. This was no time to argue with a woman. He hitched the team again, looking around hopefully for some sign of Judd, and consoling himself with the reflection that the team had cooled down and were docile enough now, after their run in from the ranch that morning.

But when she had taken her seat and given them their heads, and he saw how taut was her hold on the reins, saw the bays snort and lift their heads, necks curving, nostrils beginning to flare, he knew that the wild mood of their mistress had communicated itself to the horses through the feel of the reins. He saw them lengthen their stride, whirl out of town in a swirl of dust which lengthened along the road and hung there like a fog of approaching storm.

Shaking his head, Big Tom turned, hurrying now, leaving the stable alone. He found Judd in a saloon, moodily toying with a glass at the bar, and gave him the news crisply.

'Better get a horse and burn leather,' he advised. 'I'd have stopped her if I could—but she's drivin' now like the devil was perched on top the buggy!'

★ ★ ★

Big Tom's description was accurate enough, save that it seemed to Anticlea that the devil was in her own heart, tearing, rending with savage claws. All in one vivid blinding flash she had had the blanket of protection, in which she had long wrapped herself, torn away, seeming to leave her naked, a suddenly unlovely thing. It had been a cocoon built of shame and selfishness, and whenever a rift had threatened in it she had carefully woven it a little together, shutting her eyes and her mind to truth.

Now it was done. And she with it. Cassel had said nothing. Only looked at her. And she had seen the truth in his eyes, just as the sight of his empty sleeve had shocked her to the enormity of the thing she had done to him. Now, when it was too late, she knew the magnitude of her own mistake. That she had loved him, that she still loved him. And that, as she had discovered nearly four months ago, she had never loved Robert Yoder.

Her mind was in turmoil. Let the horses run! She could not run away from what was in her heart, but in speed and movement there seemed to be surcease, as though it would press back what was reaching out to crush her. She became aware, finally, that the speed of the bays had increased from a fast trot to a gallop, that that had changed again and that they were running away—bits in teeth, long legs stretching, heads out-thrust, ears laid back, that the light buggy was jerking and swaying, as though it would whip about and come to pieces.

She pulled back with all her strength, and

spoke, as strongly, as soothingly, as she could, and knew a moment almost of panic, for words and effort alike were useless here. Ahead was a dug-road, around the shoulder of a hill, a steep turn and bank down below. Desperately she tried to check them, and felt their speed increase with the madness engendered in them. She knew when the buggy started to lift and go, and in that moment she was no longer afraid. Almost a sense of exultation, of release, came to her. She had wished to die, and now, she thought, God was being good to her. Was granting her wish.

With the buggy twisting, going, overturning, the horses scrambled wildly, almost being dragged off the narrow road by the tugging weight of it. They kicked in a wild frenzy, and the traces tore loose, the buggy, with its passenger, went tumbling, sliding, pitching end over end, down the slope below. Bushes caught at it and were broken off or bent aside, blue service-berries and red roses alike gave a smear of juice as they were crushed in passing.

It reached the bottom, where brown buck-brush made a mat like a mattress; upside down now, two wheels hopelessly smashed. The others spun briefly, crazily, and a limp oustretched form lay half under, half clear of the wreckage, not moving, blood oozing down one white arm. The sun still made a riot in the disordered glory of her hair.

* * *

Judd had ridden hard, with that long-stretching line of slow-setting dust mockingly ahead. He had sighted the buggy, half a mile ahead, had seen how wildly the horses were running, and the curve of the dug-road, and had cursed his own helplessness, roweling his horse with pitiless heels. It had happened before his eyes, following just about the pattern he had expected.

Some of the qualities which had caused Yoder to make him his foreman emerged then. In a crisis there was no bluster or lost motion. Even the smothering feeling that had risen in him he choked down, shoved to one side while he worked with a sort of ordered frenzy.

A wagon was coming along the road, heading for town, and he stopped it, secured help. They had lifted the limp, bleeding form of Anticlea as gently as possible, gotten her into the bed of the wagon box on a clutter of old straw. And then Judd had ridden ahead again, to find the doctor and have things ready.

Then, an hour later, and with a sort of mirthless humour, he had started back for

Horseshoe again. Reflecting that it was only a few hours since he had last ridden home from Canyon, reflecting on what he could find to say to his boss, and how bitter and calamitous a thing it had seemed to him at the time—being bested and made a laughing-stock of by a one-armed man.

Now, in retrospect, that was a thing to laugh about and forget. Now he must tell Yoder of how he had failed again, and of the dreadful consequences of it. A man possessed of plenty of courage, it was only his sense of duty to his employer which kept him going now. He would rather have taken a horsewhipping than go through with this, would cheerfully have thrown up a good job and ridden anywhere else, only it was a job to be done. Moreover, he knew that he must remain until he knew whether Anticlea would live or die.

Not that he was daunted in this job by any fear of Robert Yoder, physically. Though the boss could be plenty tough on occasion. It was what he would see in Yoder's face and hear in his voice that he feared. He knew how he would feel, if Anticlea was his wife.

So, doggedly and trying without success to shut out the terrible vision of Anticlea as he had found her there beneath the wreck of the buggy, he rode for Horseshoe.

Yoder was at the house, having just returned from the range. He saw Judd coming, on horseback, and from the look on his face he knew that something was badly amiss. He took a few long strides to meet him.

'Well?' he demanded.

Judd told his story, in plain, unvarnished words, not striving, this time, to make excuses. Yoder's face tightened, but he listened without interruption until he had finished.

'How is she?' he asked then.

'Doc Gray's still workin' over her. She's unconscious, with a broken arm and no tellin' what else—' Judd hesitated, came out with the bald truth, though it seemed to stick in his throat. 'He didn't say so in so many words, but I think he figgers she'll die.'

Yoder's next question surprised and shocked him a little.

'Had she seen Cassel?'

'Danged if I know,' Judd confessed. 'I left her off at the hotel, like I said—'

'And he's stayin' there.' Yoder's eyes were hooded, filmed like a hawk's. 'So of course she had.'

'Mebby,' Judd agreed dubiously. 'Kind of doubt it though. I'd just run into him—back at the livery stable.'

Yoder's emotion, or lack of it, surprised him. He had expected an outburst, to be fired, anything but this. It came to him suddenly that Robert Yoder was not particularly concerned about what happened to his wife. His next words seemed to prove it.

'What happened there? Did you warn him to get out of the country?'

'I was aimin' to,' Judd agreed. Here was something that would shock Robert Yoder, even if this other recital had no power to.

'You *aimed* to?' Yoder repeated, a little sarcastically. 'But didn't? Are you afraid of the man?'

Judd shook his head, his jaw clamping hard.

'I was aimin' to, but I didn't,' he said. 'I figgered I'd better see you first. He was wearin' a badge—as Marshal of Bitter Creek.'

CHAPTER SIX

This time, Judd was not disappointed. He had surprised Yoder, and shocked him. Judd could see it in his eyes.

'You sure?' Yoder asked.

'A man can't be sure of nothin' in this world,' Judd said, a little sarcastically. 'But he was wearin' the marshal's badge.'

Yoder considered this, in silence. Then he nodded.

'I'll have to be getting in to town,' he said. And whether it was on account of his wife, or because of this other development, was anybody's guess.

In town, however, Yoder went directly to the *Cattleman*, where Anticlea had been taken. There was a sick room smell about the room, a sort of hushed air about the place, and he remembered in time to take off his hat and modulate his voice to a proper show of concern. He recalled then, belatedly, that he had offered no word of censure to Judd for his own negligence in letting this thing happen. Not that the man could well be blamed, apparently. But the omission on Yoder's part would be noticed.

He went in, and Anticlea lay there, still and white, in a big bed, with the odour of medicines stronger here. Kathleen stood by the foot of the bed, a soft look of pity in her eyes, but she turned to go out as Yoder entered. He stopped her with a gesture.

'How is she?' he asked.

Kathleen shook her head.

'You'll have to ask Doc Gray,' she said. 'He didn't tell me anything.'

She went out then, leaving him alone. Yoder took a turn or so, up and down the room, and then forced himself to sink down in the chair and wait. Waiting would do no good, of course. It would probably be hours, perhaps days, before Anticlea would recover consciousness, if ever. Right now, she looked as though she were dead already.

He felt a momentary pang of shame that he could think so coldly and without emotion. After all, Anticlea was his wife. But he had never wanted more than two things of her. One, the biggest and most paramount, was the ranch which she had inherited from her father, the old Window Sash. Having taken over Tincup, he really no longer needed it, but it was a key part in his plan for other ranches which lay beyond, a natural stepping-stone to possession of half the valley. With it, and the water which it controlled, he could throttle others of his neighbours. Without it, they could cause him some difficulty.

So he had attained it in the simplest way, for Anticlea had signed such papers as he had asked her to, on the day after their marriage. He didn't know yet whether she understood that she had signed Window Sash over to him, or not. She hadn't much of a head for business, as she laughingly confessed at the time.

His other reason for marrying her had been the desire, over the years, to take her away from Cassel.

But once that was done, he had lost interest. So obsessed had he been with the notion of taking her away from Cassel, and fearful, up to the last moment, that Cassel would return and he would fail, that he had been slow to see things. Slow to understand that what he felt for Kathleen Kenney was more than a passing irritation for the cool way in which she treated him . . . To understand that he loved her.

He had known that Kathleen despised him, that she laid the fault of her brother's death at his door . . . But not until he had married Anticlea had it dawned on him how he had slammed the door completely shut, and in reaching a grasping hand, had closed it on the thing of lesser value.

The silence of the room, of the big hotel, was oppressive. A big fly buzzed somewhere near the ceiling, in the shadowy part of the room, and that was the only sound. He wanted to jump up, to pace back and forth, to shout for someone else to come here and do this useless watching, so that he could be about necessary work. He'd ought to be having a talk with Paddy, right now! His brow clouded. Damn the man! He would have to pick this time to kick over the traces.

Steeling himself to calmness, his mind flicked back over the past months. Anticlea had been quick to sense his lack of interest in her. He knew that now, though he had never been at any particular pains to conceal the truth from her. It had always been his habit, when he had gotten what he wanted, to discard the instrument. Once he had ridden three hundred miles in a single stretch. He had killed two horses on the trip, good horses. But he hadn't regretted that part, for they had served the occasion.

He had seen the growth of hate in Anticlea, of late. At first she had been merely bewildered, hurt. She had tried to find out what was wrong, to make herself pleasant and attractive in his eyes. Then, as she had begun to understand, to sense the real truth, she had stopped trying. She was still pleasant on the surface, but that was just the keeping up of appearances for others to see. He had done that much himself, rather grudgingly.

Now she was lying here, injured, maybe dying—and maybe that was the best way out of it, after all. He toyed with the idea, coldly. If she should die, he'd be free again. And with the power and wealth he now possessed, the things he'd learned of late—he'd find a way to get Kathleen, too. Just as he'd found the way to get Anticlea, when she kept putting him off with the repeated insistence that she was promised to Cassel, and had to wait for him . . . If she should die.

He looked at her now, with more interest. She made a pretty picture, even now, he conceded grudgingly, with her fair hair loose on the pillow, one white arm, with a bruise showing, partly exposed, the other arm all bandaged. None of that interested him. Judd had said that she would probably die. She looked like it, right now.

There was a step, and Mrs. Kenney came

into the room. She nodded to him, and he was hard put to it to keep his voice down, to keep the irritation out of it. What was the sense, anyway, of speaking softly, when Anticlea couldn't hear a clap of thunder? But he remembered to do it, and motioned Mrs. Kenney out into the hallway.

'I'll hire somebody to look after her,' he said. 'Right away.'

'Kathleen and I will be glad to stay with her,' Mrs. Kenney said. 'And I've had some experience of nursing.'

He knew that, and it was precisely what he did not want. But he smiled and thanked her warmly.

'If it gets too dragged out, though, I'm going to get someone else to help, so that it won't be too much a burden for you,' he promised. And, going downstairs, halted abruptly at the foot. Cassel was just starting up them.

For a moment the two men fronted each other, in a quick, searching survey. Yoder's mouth tightened a little at sight of the marshal's badge pinned on Cassel's shirt. Judd had told the truth, then. Though, knowing Paddy, he hadn't doubted that any of the time.

Cassel stood aside for him to pass, not speaking. Yoder made as if to say something, changed his mind, and went swiftly across the lobby and out of doors. *Damn the man!* he thought furiously. Always, from as far back as he had known Cassel, he had felt a sense of inferiority when in his presence. Whence it sprang, or why, he could never quite account for. Certainly he was as good looking, as quick and decisive in action, and more successful in whatever he turned his hand to. He had demonstrated that, often enough. But the feeling would not down.

Now, he knew, Cassel hated him, and that was reward well earned, something to enjoy. But he felt, as he had done so many times, that this one-armed beggar who had returned to Bitter Creek, regarded him with contempt as well, and that was the thing he could not endure. It was this feeling of inferiority, which would never down, that had driven him so relentlessly to show the valley, show himself, and show Cassel, what he could do—to take away from Cassel everything which he valued or claimed for his own.

Yesterday he'd known that he had succeeded. And today the man flaunted a star in his face and looked at him with contempt!

He jerked his mind back roughly. No time to dwell on such things. There were practical things that he could do about it. And if Anticlea should really die—

It was never his way to leave things to chance. This was a perfect, golden opportunity, which might never come again. A nurse—if he could find the right one—might be the answer. He had sensed that, back when talking with Mrs. Kenney. There was one rub, however. To find a woman who would do what he wanted done, and not excite suspicion—and to get her installed as nurse. There were such women in town, to be sure. He could name enough of them, off-hand, calling each by name, to fill the fingers of both hands. For gold, or perhaps only whisky, or a little white powder, they would do the job.

But no such woman could be installed as nurse. It simply wouldn't do. Even if he was so foolish as to try it. Mrs. Kenney wouldn't allow them inside the *Cattleman.*

For an alternative, there was Doc Gray—but money wouldn't corrupt old Doc, grown grey-headed in the service of the community. Fear, even fear of death, wouldn't intimidate him. There were such men—few and far between, maybe, but, like Cassel, they existed, and could be thorny problems at times. Still, there was always some way of handling such men.

He had reached the Mercantile now, and he dismissed that problem from his mind for the moment, as he tramped in and down the aisle to the rear. Here were groceries on the one side, with their rich, pungent odours, some of them suggesting the romance of far-off places, of spice islands in tropical seas; others bringing homey smells of farm, and ranch, or the eastern city, dimly remembered, where he had lived first as a boy.

Dry goods were on the other, blankets and clothes, boots and ladies' dresses, and saddles beyond, with their conflicting, utterly different category of smells. For just a moment, taking that short walk down the length of the store, Yoder knew nostalgia, a different sort of frustration. Always, here in the Mercantile, it was like a sort of home-coming—a stepping back into a dimly-remembered past which he had never really known, but which seemed to belong to him.

If it wasn't for ambition—for his driving sense of urgency in being a big man, a bigger man than Clyde Cassel—then he might be what he had sensed would be his life, as a small boy. A clerk in such a store as this, and some day the owner.

That had been a cherished, now almost forgotten dream, until the day he had met Cassel. From then on it had begun to fade. Yet always, in this brief walk down these aisles, it haunted him. Here, pottering among such homey, down to earth things, a man could know peace and contentment.

He tramped up the stairs, nodding shortly in return to the gun-guards posted there. He did not bother to knock at the door of Paddy's office, but instead sent a short, challenging look at the guard, who nodded slightly. Yoder pushed open the door, stepped through, and closed it with a sharp thrust of his upturned boot.

As he had known would be the case, Paddy was expecting him. No man could come the length of the Mercantile and up those stairs without Paddy knowing, if it was at all important that he should. Now, looking more benevolent than usual, Paddy pushed the box of cigars towards him. His voice held a warmth which it usually lacked, and then Yoder sensed what it was—sympathy.

'I'm moighty sorry to hear the news, Robert me b'y,' Paddy said. 'And 'tis hopin' I am 'twill not be so bad as first reports have it.'

He had fooled Paddy, in this, along with most others, Yoder reflected. The man really believed that he loved his wife.

'I don't know, Paddy,' he sighed, sinking into a chair, his voice holding the proper shade of emotion. 'I've just come from there—but I haven't had a chance to talk with Doc, yet. I'm hoping, too.'

'Sure, and we'll all be doin' the same with all our hearrts,' Paddy agreed. And, that topic out of the way, both men eyed each other a little warily, sensing the real reason for this visit. Yoder chose to be blunt.

'What's this I hear about Cassel being the new marshal?' he demanded.

'Don't you think he's a good man for the

job?' Paddy asked slyly.

'A man with one arm?' Yoder's tone was contemptuous.

'Some men can do more with one arrm than others with two.'

Paddy watched him a moment, then probed slyly.

'And besides, he being an old fri'nd of yours, Robert—and havin' had the misfortune to lose Tincup, I thought ye'd be glad to have me turn somethin' his way.'

'You know damned well that I want him run out of the country,' Yoder said impatiently. 'And so you do that. What for?'

Paddy's shoulders shook with suppressed mirth.

'Maybe because I like to do such things,' he suggested.

'In other words, you're breakin' our truce?'

'I didn't say that.'

'You might as well.' Yoder stood up impatiently, and his face was tight and ugly. 'There always comes a time when two big men get to pushing too strongly against each other, Paddy. I'm not breakin' our truce—but I'm warnin' you. If you're starting something, it's all right with me. And I'll finish it!'

'Maybe you will, Robert,' Paddy agreed. 'Maybe.' His voice did not rise, became even a little softer, but subtle with menace. 'But be damned sure ye can, before ye turn your dogs loose!'

CHAPTER SEVEN

Cassel met Kathleen at the head of the stairs. At the question in his eyes, she shook her head.

'There's no change—yet. Mother's with her, now.'

She went on downstairs, treading softly on the carpet which had replaced the bare clatter of rough boards since the Kenneys had taken over the *Cattleman,* and Cassel stood to look after her for a moment, watching her go almost with reluctance. There was a quiet sympathy which emanated from her which could not be mistaken. She was a warm, comfortable woman—a motherly sort, just like his own mother had been. Somehow it disturbed him, for he had condemned all women alike in his mind, only the day before—damning them along with all men. In her, he sensed that there was contradiction to such a sweeping generality.

He paused at the door of the sick room for a moment, as he had done twice earlier since Anticlea had been brought there, and his face, under its heavy beard, softened a little more. It was hard to remember that cold, remorseless letter which Anticlea had written him, to think of how she had betrayed his trust in her, marrying the man who had desecrated Tincup and his mother's old home—where Anticlea had played as a child—as Robert Yoder had done.

Lying there, she looked so helpless, and somehow so appealing, that he could remember only the old Anticlea, and bitterness washed out of him, leaving him curiously empty. Whatever happened, she was still Yoder's wife, and that was that. But for the rest, he couldn't hate nor even condemn her—not now.

She was likely to die, without ever regaining consciousness. Doc Gray had been a long-time friend of his—one of the few who had greeted him as heartily to-day, after four years, as though he was still a whole man, and owner of a greater Tincup and all the rest. Doc had looked at his empty sleeve and mumbled deep in his own beard which reached to his chest, but his handclasp had been strong, and his eyes moist.

'It's too early to be sure, but from what Judd told me, of the way she was, with that buggy on top of her, and what I can find—I'm afraid she's busted up pretty bad inside,' he had said bluntly. 'If that's the case—it's beyond any such poor skill as I have. 'Tis only the good God can save her now, and He, knowin' what He does, might think that no kindness to her.'

That last cryptic remark had set Cassel thinking. Somehow, he had taken it for granted that, having married Yoder, Anticlea would be happy. Now he knew that would not be so. There was a charm and magnetism about Yoder, unquestionably. But he charmed with it as a snake charms a bird. Behind the power which drew would be the thrall of terror. No one, least of all Anticlea, could be long happy with such a man. And if she married him for his possessions, that must be doubly so.

The keen-eyed doctor had sensed that, evidently. And her own words to him, that poignant cry before she had rushed away, was proof enough. Cassel shook his head. Maybe Doc Gray was right. Maybe God would take her home as being the greater kindness. Yet, seeing her so limp and helpless, the beauty of her, knowing the vivid spirit that dwelt in her body, it seemed a pitiful thing to contemplate.

He was in his room when a knock came at the door, and a messenger handed him a note. It was a brief scrawl, in Paddy's characteristic handwriting.

'Come to my room this evening, as soon as you've had supper. Important.'

He wondered a little as to what that would mean, and noticed that he had sat overlong, musing on the past. Already it was growing dusk outside, the outlines of the hills which compassed Canyon were vague and formless. The town was beginning to stir to real activity now. This was Saturday, and families were coming to town for their weekly shopping, cowboys coming in for a chance to wash the dust of a long week from their throats. The streets were crowded, mostly by men he had never seen before. For the next half-dozen hours, Canyon would be more astir than in all the rest of the week combined.

Cassel went to a restaurant and got his supper. He knew that Kathleen intended that he should eat with them in their own little kitchen, and having thought it over, he preferred the idea too. They were doing it, Kathleen and her mother, to give him a touch of home and of good food, well cooked—a welcome to Bitter Creek, partly in atonement for what others here had done to him, partly in place of Kathleen's own brother, who would not be returning.

His acceptance would please them, and he could pay extra, which he knew would help them. For there was not enough business at the hotel to make it a paying proposition. Yoder's altruism had not extended that far. He had gotten out of one obligation by palming off a white elephant. They did the work themselves, and had a living, but that was all.

But tonight, with Anticlea to be looked after and routine all upset, he sought the restaurant, noting with a detached amusement the difference in the quality of the food. The meal ended, he turned toward the *Palace*, which was a combination of saloon and hotel. Much business that had formerly gone to the *Cattleman*, when it possessed a bar, turned now to the *Palace*.

There was an outside stairs, of rough, silvery planking, unpainted, with a hand rail of two-by-four, and he climbed that, let himself into the long hall, and saw a gleam of light under a door at the far end, knew from what he had been told that this would be Paddy's room. A lounging shadow moved in the gloom, a hoarse voice came to his ears.

'Who is it?'

He smiled faintly to himself, for here was one of Paddy's gun-guards. What must it be like to possess power, and to go always in fear of one's life, constantly under the need of men watchful to try and kill an enemy before they could get him in turn? He gave his name, and rapped at the door, and Paddy opened it for him.

Paddy's office, above the Mercantile, was an ornate affair, and fitted with costly stuff. That Cassel guessed, was calculated to impress visitors to his place of business. It did not represent the real Paddy or his tastes.

Here, where he slept, Paddy was as unpretentious as in the days when he had been a tramp, with only a roadside tree or bush for his roof, the soft earth for couch. The room could be any one of the other rooms in this hotel, no better, no worse. It was not half so comfortable or homelike as the rooms at the *Cattleman*, since Kathleen and her mother had transformed them with a deft womanly touch here and there.

'Take the chair, me b'y,' Paddy urged hospitably. 'Or set ye on the bed if ye loike, 'twould no doubt be softer. Pah, 't is a warrm avenin', and this room is stuffy.'

He crossed impatiently to the window, jerked up the shade—kept drawn, Cassel guessed, for reasons of safety—then raised the window with a jerk as well. The cool night air which flowed in was a welcome change from the stuffiness which had prevailed.

'I just got here,' Paddy apologised. He set to one side the coal-oil lamp on the little table, searched ineffectually for something, and shook his head.

'Not here,' he said. 'But no matter.' Cassel having taken the chair, Paddy seated himself on the edge of the bed, which creaked protestingly under his weight. 'Ye're wondering what I sent for ye for, av course.'

'No. I'd been wondering why you didn't,' Cassel retorted.

Paddy smiled and shook his head.

'As I told ye this mornin', Clyde me b'y, there are no strings attached to your job. Ye may figure it strange that a man loike mesilf, who ye remimber as a tramp, and who has run the town by being a law unto mesilf, should get to the point where law and dacency should have an appeal. But 't is so. 'T is what I want for Canyon—and for Bitter Creek. If ye can give it to them, there are no conditions.'

'You're being more than fair,' Cassel admitted.

'I figure 't is toime someone was, with ye,' Paddy said shrewdly. 'And a man gets farther with fr'inds who trust him—and loike him—than whin he has to hire for money those who guard his worthless carcass. Gold can buy, and gold can corrupt.' He laughed shortly, mirthlessly. 'Sure, and sometoimes I wonder is it worrth it all. Far happier was I with niver a cent to me name and free as the birrds, and no man hatin' me nor thirstin' for me blood.'

He was leading up to something, Cassel saw, but doing it in his own way. This was a new side to Paddy, however—a side which was revealed to few men.

'Ye know, av course, that Horseshoe aims to run ye out av the country—or kill ye?' Paddy asked suddenly.

'That's about to be expected,' Cassel agreed.

'I've passed the worrd, this avenin', to me min, that ye being the law, they back ye up—in whativer comes along,' Paddy added.

'Moind ye, Clyde me b'y, it's you who'll call the tune. But 't is foine, now and agin, to have some one to dance whin ye pipe.'

'I appreciate that, Paddy,' Cassel assured him.

''T is only common sinse on me part,' Paddy shrugged. 'Ye're still wonderin' why I'm doing this. I loike to see a man get a square deal—when it suits me purposes. But I'm not bein' altruistic. Not me. Did ye know all the truth now, I have small doubt ye'd hate me.'

'You mean, because you've been working with Yoder?'

Paddy grimaced. He was seated back in the shadow, and puffing at a short, black pipe, smoking a vile tobacco. The smoke eddied and wreathed about his curling silvery locks, giving him more than ever the appearance of a benign preacher.

'Say instead, that I've been holdin' him from his full ambition,' he said. 'But there's still too much truth in it. Mind ye now, Clyde me b'y, I'm makin' no promises—some things belong to the future. But 't is a wise man that takes precautions in the presint. So 't is that I want ye to know where I kape certain papers. Just in case. But first, on your word of honour—and I know ye for a man of honour—I want your promise not to pry among them so long as I am runnin' me own affairs. For I still loike to have ye for a fr'ind.'

'You have my word,' Cassel agreed readily.

'And I appreciate that, Clyde. How much, mebby one day ye'll know. Right now—'

He stood up, turned towards the table. It happened in that same moment, as though someone had been waiting with an unyielding patience. The rifle crashed from somewhere in the blackness of the night, the bullet clipped through both panes of window glass, where the one was raised to a level with the other. One crashed shatteringly, but all these things came to Cassel as sort of background impressions.

For Paddy was suddenly swaying on his feet, a red gush of crimson welling out from his mouth. He swayed, clutching at the edge of the table to steady himself. He missed his hold, crashed and lay sprawled grotesquely on the floor, even while the echoes of the shot still rang among the hills beyond.

CHAPTER EIGHT

A small section of the window glass dropped with a light tinkle on the floor. A breath of evening breeze came in at the open window, wind down from the hills beyond, rich with the fruity fragrance of harvest. The lamp wavered in the breeze, the light flickering grotesquely.

Cassel reached it with a sidling motion which lost no time, but kept him out of direct range from the window. He puffed a breath at it, and darkness was like spilled ink overflowing the room. Cassel drew the shade, and it slipped as he released it, zipped suddenly to the top of the window again with a whirr of uncoiling spring, jerked itself violently loose and fell to the floor.

And from the dark of the alleys beyond, the rifle barked a second time, more glass tinkled and fell.

The killer, posted out there, was after the two of them equally. A man precise, machine-like in operation, and therefore doubly dangerous. Fists pounded on the door now, the hoarsely urgent voice of the gun-guard demanded to know what was happening.

'Wait,' Cassel ordered, and opened the door. He stepped through, into the hall, feeling the quivering nervousness of the man beside him, like a hound held on leash while a fox escaped with a chicken in its mouth.

'Somebody shot Paddy,' Cassel explained. 'Get a blanket to put over that window—the shade's broken. Then get the doctor. I'm going to try and find the fellow that did the shooting.'

'Wait a minute,' the other man said urgently. 'If Paddy's been shot, how do I know that you didn't do it?'

'Try lighting the lamp in there, and find out,' Cassel suggested grimly. He reached the stairway, and saw that a shaft of moonlight lay half across it, part way down. Hesitating only an instant, he went to the edge of the roof, grasping at it with the fingers of his own hand, lowered himself and let go.

His feet plunged through old weeds, crunched a rusty tin can flat into the ground. The scent of ragweed filled the air, tickling his nostrils, and he fought against an impulse to sneeze. Then, keeping in the deeper patch of shadow thrown by the building, he moved swiftly in the direction whence the shots had come.

Horseshoe was losing no time. Whether it was Robert Yoder, or Judd, or more probably both together, the result was the same. Whatever truce had existed between Yoder and Paddy was ended now, since Paddy had seen fit to join forces with him. This was war—war to the death.

The shots had attracted no particular attention in Canyon. Drunken cowboys, in town for Saturday night, were accustomed to firing a few wild shots by way of celebration. There had been scarcely a break in the even tempo of the evening. Gun-fire was less than the barking of a dog.

His own gun was in his hand now, and the solid butt of the army revolver had an easy, familiar feel. There had been a time when such a nocturnal foray made his palm wet with sweat, quickened his breath a little; a time when it had always seemed to him as though there was lead in the pit of his stomach, and a tightened feeling like colic all through him. That was all gone now. He was steady, as deadly a stalker as any animal loose in the bush. A ruthless man, he reflected sourly, and too late, of course.

Ahead of him was where the killer had waited. It was the only good spot whence he could have seen that window and lined his rifle on it, without being seen himself. A sort of half-alley, half-pocket, where three buildings had been set like blocks, forming an open U. The opening was at the rear of all three, and in that, and comfortably in the dark, the killer had waited.

But not too long. He had slipped away, no telling where. By now he could be out of town, or innocently guzzling a beer in any of the bars. Or he might be lurking in the shadows close at hand.

A brass-jacketed shell gleamed in the rays of the moon. The shell of a regulation army rifle, Cassel saw, as he picked it up. Newly-fired, with the warm smell of powder still odorous about it. Not much of a clue, for while this was undoubtedly the shell that had sent its lead into Paddy, still there were plenty such rifles everywhere, these days. It had been ejected as a fresh shell was levered in to be fired at him, of course.

It was too dark to see anything more, and Cassel retreated carefully, knowing that to prowl now might ruin any evidence which would show in daylight. He found the *Palace* astir with lights now, humming with activity. News of the shooting had spread, and in the lobby he encountered the gun-guard who had been in the dark hall upstairs. A tall, gangly man with a pendulous lower lip which was habitually stuffed with snuff, and who went by the name of Rusty.

'How's Paddy?' Cassel asked.

'Hard hit,' was the retort. 'He's alive—but that's about all. Doc Gray's had him moved to the *Cattleman*. Though why, I dunno.'

Cassel could guess. The *Cattleman* was not far off, and it was a quieter place for a sick man, and likewise, there was Kathleen Kenney and her mother. Ample reason in a town with such powerfully opposing cross-currents as this.

Kathleen met him in the lobby, grave-eyed. She carried a basin with its water stained crimson.

'Doc Gray is with him now,' she explained. 'He's alive—that's all I know. But it looks pretty bad.'

Cassel could understand that. A rifle bullet, hitting a man at close range, was bad medicine. Even if Paddy survived the effect of the bullet itself, he would be up in turn against an even deadlier foe—a killer which Cassel had seen, times without number, on the battlefield. Infection. It had killed more men than all the bullets the enemy had fired, had been able to do, put together.

Impatience stirred in him. He took a lantern and went out again. Back at the U formed by the three buildings, he lit it, looked around more carefully. His eyes lightened. Someone had thrown slops from one of the buildings. So that the ground back here, mostly shaded all day long as it was, was soggy, soft, almost muddy. Probably in the darkness the gunman hadn't noticed that or given it a second thought.

But he had left the imprint of hob-nailed boots here. There were plenty of hob-nailed boots in this country, but there could scarcely be another pair to match these. For size, they were the biggest things that Cassel had ever seen. It would take a huge man, like Big Tom, to wear such shoes.

And the pattern of the hob-nails was irregular, distinctive. On one boot they had been driven, purely by chance, so that they formed a rough U as well.

'If I ever see the bottom of that boot, there'll be no mistaking it,' Cassel reflected, and blew out the lantern. It was getting close to midnight, and the town, probably sobered by the news of what had happened to Paddy, was quieting before its usual time. Half of the saloons were dark already, the horses at hitch rails and tied to trees had thinned to a few scattered, sleepy nags. Cassel went to the livery stable. It would still be doing business, a few last teams going out and homeward.

A coal-oil lamp burned in the little office, with the door standing open. Big Tom, idle for the moment, lounged there, a straw in his mouth. He removed it to greet Cassel, and the latter glancing floorward, saw that Big Tom, for all the great size of him, wore a small, high-heeled boot.

'Evenin', Marshal,' Big Tom nodded. 'They tell me Paddy's been shot?' He looked keenly as Cassel. 'You was there?'

'Right in the same room,' Cassel agreed.

'Did the first shot get him?' Big Tom asked bluntly.

'Yes.'

'And there was two shots,' the stableman said ruminatively. 'Course, as his marshal, you'll be sorta unpopular—'

He left it at that, the words trailing off into nothingness. But Cassel liked him. If he knew anything about men, Big Tom was one to trust. And he had to trust somebody now.

'You're a big man, Tom, to have such small feet,' he suggested.

Big Tom looked down at his feet, and grinned. But there was sudden shrewdness in his eyes.

'All a man needs is feet big enough to stand

on,' he said. 'I've seen some that'd have been big men, like me, if they hadn't all run to feet.'

'Such as?' Cassel probed.

'Well, there's two—they ain't exactly runts, but they sure got a right solid foundation. Dutton's one. Runs the post office.'

'Who got him appointed?'

'Paddy.'

'And the other one?'

'That other feller, he must've been quite a button, 'fore his parents could tell which way he was going to walk,' Big Tom grinned. 'He's mostly called the Fox hereabouts—Reynal's his name. Horseshoe.'

Big Tom turned away, as another man came and wanted his horse, and Cassel returned to the *Cattleman*. Big Tom had indicated clearly his own suspicion that if the killer was big-footed, that he would be one of these two men, and Reynal—the Fox—would be a gunman, of course.

Doc Gray, looking tired, was just finishing a cup of hot coffee and lunch which Mrs. Kenney had prepared for him. He smiled at Cassel as he came in.

'Fine time to be drinking coffee, at one o'clock in the morning, eh?' he asked. 'Always keeps me awake—and I'd like to sleep. But I've just got a call, so coffee helps. And thank you, Mrs. Kenney. You're an angel. You and Kathleen both.'

He yawned, pushed back his chair, and stood up. Cassel looked a question. Doc Gray stooped to pick up his bag, and shook his head.

'He's sleeping now—I gave him something to put him to sleep,' he said. 'He was suffering pretty badly. Bullet sure tore up his face plenty. Well, I'll know more in the morning—if he's still alive by then.'

He clapped Cassel on the shoulder, nodding.

'Better get some sleep, Marshal. And keep away from lighted windows!'

That was excellent advice, Cassel knew. It warmed him that these people should show a friendly interest in him. None of those he had known in the old days, aside from Doc Gray, had been very friendly. But Doc made up for a lot of others. And Big Tom, Mrs. Kenney, Kathleen—

She was in the upper hall as he climbed the stairs. She looked tired, but he knew that she was staying awake, keeping watch in both sick rooms. Not that there was much to do. Both patients were asleep—or deep in unconsciousness. Rusty had taken up his stand in Paddy's room, in a chair, tipped back against the wall.

He saw that there was concern in Kathleen's eyes as she looked at him, after he had glanced in the room.

'I understand that the killer tried to get you, too,' she said.

Cassel made light of it.

'I happened to be there,' he said. 'And then, of course, he'll be leery of the law.'

'That's not it,' Kathleen replied soberly. 'You know it's not. It's you.'

'Even if I do wear a star now, I'm not so dreadful as to excite such suspicion. At least, not until I've done something.'

'I don't think that your wearing a star has much to do with it,' she insisted. 'Canyon's always been rough—even pretty wild, at times. But you've been here less than two days, and things have changed. There's a whole new atmosphere, somehow.'

'You mean, I'm sort of a stormy petrel?'

'Maybe.' She considered him soberly. 'You remind me of a hill, near where I lived as a little girl. It was the highest point of land anywhere around there. A craggy sort of a place.'

'And I'm craggy and unlovely, too. I guess you're right.'

'That wasn't what I meant. You're like the hill in one way—you stand head and shoulders above nearly everyone else. I don't know just why, but you do. Everyone feels it. And what I was going to say is that you're like that hill in another way. Whenever there was a storm, it always seemed to attract lightning.'

'Maybe I'd ought to get a room somewhere else,' Cassel suggested. 'For I guess you're right. I do attract lightning.'

'It's you I'm thinking of,' Kathleen insisted. 'I wouldn't want to see you—like Paddy, or Anticlea. So—so white and helpless. But we wouldn't want you to go anywhere, Mother and I—not on our account.'

'I'll stay, if you like,' he agreed. 'It's the nicest place I've struck in years.' He felt curiously warmed as he let himself into his own room. Then his thoughts grew sober. Doc Gray's warning, not to stand in the light. And Kathleen's comment that he seemed to draw lightning.

He slept soundly, and awoke to be told that there was no change in Anticlea. Nor, so far as Mrs. Kenney knew, in Paddy. But Doc Gray was with him again. The door opened, and Doc beckoned to him, closed the door again as he entered the room.

Rusty still lounged in a chair at the side, unobtrusively out of the way. Paddy was awake. Cassel could tell that. Awake, and looking at him with great, questioning eyes, above his bandaged face. In them was a deep-seated pain. Doc's voice was a little hoarse.

'He's conscious,' he said. 'And putting up a good fight. Maybe he'll pull through.' His voice dropped. 'The devil of it is—his jaw's shattered. And that's not the worst. The bullet went through the lower part of his face, and it's hit something back in there—interferin' with the spinal cord and so on—and paralyzin' him. He can't move, or speak.'

CHAPTER NINE

Bright sunshine was flooding the town again, turning Bitter Creek to molten silver. Robert Yoder, having breakfasted well and made a duty call at the *Cattleman*, in the course of which a dry sense of humour induced him to look in on Paddy as well, he now passed out into the sunshine, with difficulty keeping a properly grave face turned to the world.

Rusty had just been leaving, being replaced by a new guard, Quantrell by name, a little man with an itchy trigger-finger and an inordinate liking for beer. The two had regarded him sourly, much to Yoder's amusement. Seeing Paddy flat on his back and helpless had increased it.

It was a good day to be alive! Never had he felt more like whistling, or doing some wild, tomboyish sort of thing such as he had not indulged in for long years. To be a power in the community—or, more accurately, the Power, a man had to present a strong, silent front to the public at all times, to let them understand that he was one with whom there could be no trifling, ever. A code which he had practised so rigorously that it had become almost second-nature now.

But things were going even better than he had expected. He had known sharp annoyance, a few moments of concern, at the return of Cassel to Bitter Creek, and Paddy's own derisive gesture to himself in making Cassel marshal. There had been the smell of trouble in the air, pungent and all-pervading as when a skunk wandered in the vicinity.

Now he knew that it was a good thing. The coming of Cassel had forced his hand, putting an end to this uneasy truce with Paddy, which had seriously hampered his plans for expansion of late. He still knew a twinge of uneasiness as he considered the thing which had induced him to accept that truce in the first place, but he brushed it aside now. Paddy was likely to die. But whether he lived or died, he was disposed of. Paralyzed, unable to walk, to talk, or move even a hand. In that knowledge was the sweet savour of vengeance such as Yoder had never dared hope for.

That took care of Paddy. Cassel could be handled when the time came. And this morning, Yoder knew how to accomplish the rest of his purpose. He had been properly crushed, talking to Kathleen and her mother, a perfect example of the distressed husband. He had seen a softening in Kathleen's eyes, a slight relenting in her attitude towards himself. She believed now that he loved his wife, that he was stricken. Before he was through playing out this act, she would almost think kindly of him.

And that would be a long step in the right direction. He was on fire now with the thought of her. What a fool he'd been, not to recognise long since that it was her he loved! He'd certainly bungled things there, and badly, he admitted wryly. She had scorned him, repelled his advances. And, still intent on marrying Anticlea and taking her away from Cassel, he hadn't been able to understand his own feelings. Yes, he'd made a ghastly mistake.

But now it was being rectified. Anticlea's illness would serve him doubly. And once he was a widower, and a proper interval of time had passed, he could appeal even more deeply to Kathleen's sympathy.

As for Anticlea and the problem which she posed, he had found a way. It looked now as though, despite her injuries, she might live, and in time recover. That was a chance he couldn't afford to take. True, if he let her live, and decided to allow Cassel to live as well, there might be a measure of revenge in the situation. But it was too dangerous an idea to toy with. She had to die, now that she was ill.

Yoder's mind was like the nest of a pack-rat, in one respect. Everything he found was packed off and stored away there for possible future use. And it was surprising how many odd and apparently useless items could be fitted into a useful pattern, sooner or later.

Six weeks ago, he had journeyed to the town of Dead Man's Creek, off across the mountains. Spending the night there, he had found entertainment in one of the saloons. With a girl who called herself Rose LaVelle. He remembered her very well. Women like her didn't often work in such places. She was distinctly above that sort of a life. And able to play the part that he desired now.

He had remembered her for two reasons. She had been distinctly better company than he had expected, a woman to remember. And, a bit intrigued by her obvious background, he had inquired as to why and how she came to be in such a place, and she had told him.

At the time, he had half-doubted whether she told the truth. About coming west in search of a long-lost brother, mostly because of a sick mother who was eating her heart out because no word ever came from that favourite son. The boy, Yoder gathered, had been pretty wild, even as a youth. But with some qualities which had endeared him to his mother and sister.

He had listened more closely, a little startled when she had gone on to describe him more particularly. And he had promised her that he would keep his eyes open, in case he ever ran across the man.

Returning to Horseshoe, he had quietly investigated the notion that had come to him then. It had taken him less than a week to make sure that he did know her brother, that the man was working for him on Horseshoe. That had been accomplished without arousing any suspicion in her brother's mind.

For the next several weeks he had let the thing drift, save for the precaution of writing one letter to Rose, telling her that he thought he had a clue. The thing had remained stored away, pack-rat wise, in a corner of his mind. It might be useful, later on.

Now he knew how to use it. Not as he had envisaged before, remembering Rose. Quite the contrary. Here was everything fitted precisely to his need. A woman who could survive in town, fitted to play the part of an eminently respectable nurse. Rose had the training and background to be accepted at the *Cattleman* for that.

And he had the information to guarantee that she would play the part as he wanted it played!

Going back to his own hotel room, in the *Palace*, he wrote a letter, sealed it, and, walking down the street to the post office, casually dropped it through the letter-slot. There would be the west-bound stage going through town in about an hour. Dutton, the postmaster, would gather up the mail within another quarter of an hour, as a matter of usual routine.

There was just one more detail to be attended to. Yoder prided himself on his careful attention to details. It was that which made his plans work so well.

Judd, he knew, would be in town again by now, after spending the night at the ranch. Judd, though he had no suspicion that his employer knew it, was Rose LaVelle's missing brother. And it was necessary that he should be out of town when Rose arrived, and for at least a couple of days thereafter.

Yoder found him down the street at the door of the Mercantile.

'Judd,' he said, 'I've got a job for you. I bought a hundred head of cattle a while back, over by Red Butte. Ensrud's place. I want you to go over there and get them. You can make it to-day, and start back in the mornin'. Take a couple of men along to help.'

'Sure,' Judd agreed, unsuspicious. Such a job was routine, and should more properly fall to the lot of such men as Brager or Baby-Face. But if the boss wanted him to do it, that made no particular difference to him.

When Yoder turned back, the stage was

just pulling out of town. He smiled a little to himself, turned into a saloon. On the strength of that he felt that he deserved a drink.

* * *

Reynal was aptly nicknamed the Fox. He was, as Big Tom had put it, a man who seemed all to have run to feet—one who might have been quite a man otherwise. But as it was, he was only five and a half feet in height, even in the big hob-nailed boots which he wore, and he seemed fox-like, crafty, in all that he did. His hair was a fox-like red. As a gunman, Yoder counted him the equal of Judd. Along with Brager and Baby-Face, these four made up his most trusted quartette of chore-men. Like Judd, Reynal had several notches on his gun.

Following his brief and unsatisfactory conference with Paddy the day before, Yoder had found Reynal and given him his instructions. Reynal had carried them out to the letter. He had hoped to get a good shot at Cassel while he was about it, but the big thing, for the moment, was to get Paddy, and when he saw them carrying Paddy out of the *Palace* on a stretcher, he knew that he had done a good job.

Most men would have mingled boldly with the crowd then in one of the saloons, or have ridden out of town. Reynal did neither. He followed that course which had earned him his nickname, and, slipping into the livery stable when no one was looking, he had climbed the ladder into the hay loft and burrowed comfortably back among the hay, bedded down for the night.

He had been just dozing off to sleep when Cassel's voice, mingled with Big Tom's, had startled him to wakefulness. It had been impossible to hear all that was said, but he had gleaned snatches which kept him awake for a long time, then allowed him to sink, still bewildered, into an uneasy sleep.

He had been still irritable and uneasy when he awoke and slipped quietly out. And then, finally, with a sort of shock, the puzzle had fitted into place in his mind, and those snatches of talk made sense.

Cassel had found where he had crouched to fire the shot, of course—and that talk about big feet—

The Fox lost no time in returning to the scene of his crime. His face twisted unpleasantly as the full light of day revealed the soft ground, the imprint of his big boots. Full understanding came to him. And a wave of apprehension along with it.

The new marshal had certainly lost no time. By now he had a pretty good idea who the killer was. Still—a crafty light crept into Reynal's eyes—Cassel hadn't caught him, yet, with these hob-nailed boots on. Maybe this could be worked out.

It was some time later that Dutton, the postmaster, just starting to reach for the letters which had been dropped into the slot-box, was startled at a voice from inside his private room of the post office, behind him. Reynal's voice.

'I want a word with you, Dutton—pronto!'

Dutton turned, paling a little. His first thought was of a mail robbery. He knew Reynal, and distrusted him completely. But the man was a gunman, and he obeyed the summons and went with him.

'Take off yore boots!' Reynal ordered. 'I'm tradin' with yuh!'

'My boots?' Dutton echoed. 'W-what for? I don't want to trade.'

'Mebby yuh don't, but I do. I got to do a long job of ridin' to-day,' Reynal added more reasonably. 'And there's a nail in one of these. I ain't got time to get it fixed. You have. And you've the only boots that'll fit me. I'm buying yours—and leavin' you mine, extra.' He pulled off his own boots, flipped a gold eagle on to the table beside them. The mark of a Horseshoe man, for Yoder always paid with gold coins. 'That ought to be fair enough.'

'Why—why sure, I guess it is, if that's the way you put it,' Dutton agreed, pocketing the coin and accepting, with less reluctance, the heavy hob-nailed boots. The reason seemed valid enough, and it wasn't nearly so bad as he had feared.

By the time he had the boots laced in place, however, it was too late to pick up the mail in the drop-box for the stage that day.

★   ★   ★

Doc Gray, having snatched a few hours of sleep during the early morning, was his calmly professional self again when he returned to the *Cattleman*. Paddy he found unchanged, and his eyes misted a little. He'd never had much use for the town boss, though he'd always found him pleasant-spoken and friendly enough. And, as between Paddy and Robert Yoder, he rather preferred Paddy.

But now he felt sorry for the man. With any luck, it looked as if the man might live and even recover from his wound, bad as it was. But if he did, the odds were still ninety-nine to one that he would remain paralyzed and helpless. When something happened to the spine, that was worse than any wound of the flesh.

Far better, Doc felt, if his skill did not avail, in such a case. Yet it was up to him, with his Hyppocratic oath and all the rest of that thing called conscience, to take the long chance and do the best he could.

He answered Quantrell's questions briefly,

wishing that Rusty was on guard instead, though Rusty was a better man for night duty, more trustworthy and apt to stay awake. Every so often, Quantrell had to slip out and across the street to the *Palace* for a glass of beer. He might as well stay there, in Doc's dour opinion. A gun-guard wasn't much use to a man in Paddy's shape.

It was a relief to pass to Anticlea's room, though she was little changed. She still lay unconscious, and it was that which worried him. He needed to do something here, wanted to do something, and was baffled by lack of skill to do it.

'Maybe, if she had a little stimulant of the right kind, it *might* work, to help her,' he reflected dubiously. And he considered it soberly. Then, as Yoder came to visit his wife, Doc Gray unburdened himself.

'I've nothing like that here,' he said. 'But I can write for it—and get it back in three-four days. Maybe it'll help—maybe not. But I think it's worth taking the chance.'

'By all means,' Yoder agreed instantly. 'Don't worry about the expense. Do anything you can, man.'

'I'll send the order out by to-morrow's stage west,' Doc Gray agreed, and felt that in the past he had perhaps done Yoder an injustice. It was plain that the man did care for his wife, despite everything.

Yoder, going outside a little later, smiled to

himself. He had put that over with the old sawbones—and Kathleen had heard it, too. Let Gray write for anything he wanted. If it didn't arrive, that would even everything.

Finding Reynal, Yoder explained briefly what he wanted.

'To-morrow's stage will have a letter, from Doc Gray,' he said. 'You'll stop the stage, and get that mail-sack. And destroy that letter!'

'Sure,' Reynal agreed. 'Only—that's kinda serious business—holdin' up the United States mail!'

'You've already done things the law would like to hang you for,' Yoder reminded him coldly. 'So one more shouldn't matter!'

Reynal considered the man for a moment, and knew, as he had long since realised, how hopelessly trapped he was. He shrugged.

'What about the rest of the mail?' he asked.

Yoder shrugged in turn.

'Throw it away—anything,' he said. 'It's of no importance.'

CHAPTER TEN

In Canyon, all business closed, as nearly as possible, on Sunday. That had been Paddy's idea, rather surprisingly. Saloons might stay open well past midnight on Saturday, but once the Sabbath began, they stayed shut. It was this factor which caused Kathleen to call to Cassel as he returned to the *Cattleman* on Sunday evening.

'Would you mind going over to the Mercantile and getting some clean white cloth for bandages?' she asked him. 'Paddy's wound has been bleeding quite a lot—and we've nothing to use here unless we tear up some sheets. Mr. Kellogg is manager of the store, and he lives at the rear. He'll open up to get whatever you want, especially if it's for Paddy.'

'Of course, I'll be glad to get some,' Cassel agreed. He looked at her with new intentness. 'Isn't this job getting to be too much for you and your mother?'

'It keeps us busy,' Kathleen admitted. 'But that's all right. Mr. Yoder says he is sending for a lady he knows about, who has done a good deal of nursing, to come and help us out. He really seems quite concerned.'

The incongruity about such a remark was that it should be made at all, but it seemed not to strike Kathleen. Cassel stepped out into the darkness. There were few lights tonight, and scarcely anyone on the streets. Sime Kellogg was a bachelor and he lived in a couple of rooms beneath the balcony of the Merc where Paddy had his office. There was no light here, either, and no response to Cassel's knock at the rear door.

He hesitated a moment, tried the door, and found it unlocked. As he stepped across the threshold he knew that something was wrong. The room was in a wild disorder, and he realised, from the little that he had seen of Sime Kellogg, with his thinning hair carefully slicked back to cover his scalp, and the waxed points of his moustache, that he would be almost painfully neat and orderly, especially in his living quarters.

Heavy, uneven breathing came from somewhere, and then he saw that it was Kellogg himself who lay there in a corner, huddled awkwardly. He was tied hand and foot, and a gag was in his mouth. But even when Cassel had removed the gag, his eyes remained closed, his breathing heavy. A swelling lump on the back of his head explained why.

'Somebody knocked him over the head, then tied him up,' Cassel muttered, and listening, heard a sound now from above-stairs. Leaving the manager in a more comfortable position, he moved on through, into the store itself, and toward the stairs leading up to the balcony.

A quick suspicion came to him of what was transpiring. Robbery—but not directed at the Mercantile. Paddy's office was the goal to-night. Keeping to the edge of the stairway, he went up it, and one step creaked loudly. The big, silent store loomed like a room full of ghosts, where hams, brooms, clothing and assorted items were suspended grotesquely from the beams above.

Nothing happened and he reached the floor above. A gleam of light came from under the office door, but it went out suddenly as he approached, and he knew that he had been heard. He flattened himself at the side as the door opened, the reek of half-burned oil coming from the sudden blowing out of the lamp.

A man stood framed, darkly, in the doorway for a moment, then stepped through. Cassel could see the faint shine of gathered light on the barrel of the gun he held. He waited until he saw the gun better, saw that it was loosely held, and then his voice lashed out.

'Drop your gun and raise your hands! I've got you covered!'

There was a startled grunt, a momentary hesitation, then the gun thudded on the floor.

'Who the devil are you?' the man demanded.

'This is the law speakin',' Cassel warned. 'Keep 'em high!'

He advanced then, and what happened came as a shock. Something hit him from the side and behind, and he realised, too late, that there had been two men in that room, that one had slipped out at a side door and circled, while the other held him in parley.

His own lack of familiarity with the place was a handicap now, and a gun-barrel had slammed at him, a murderous blow which raked the side and back of his head, as though a flaming match had been drawn along it.

It sent him staggering, his knees buckling, while a crimson glare seemed to explode inside his head. Had it been fairly delivered, he'd be out cold—or worse. But again the dark had been deceptive, and the blow had been miscalculated. Even so, he could feel the hot gush of warm blood which bubbled through the gash as he went down.

Instantly, one of the two men was flinging himself on top of him. But Cassel was ready by now, twisting over on his back, getting a fresh grip on himself. The margin by which he had missed being knocked out was enough in which to fight.

There was desperate urgency about the two of them, and that haste was to his advantage. As the man landed on him, fingers questing for his throat, Cassel brought up his left knee in a sudden jolting blow which caught the man above him full in the stomach. It flung him half off, gasping and with the wind knocked out of him, but by then the second man, who had swiped him from behind with the gun-barrel, was trying to get at him.

A strong breath breathed into his face, a fetid blend of whisky and garlic and other odours no more palatable, and the gun-barrel was raised for another chopping blow. But this time Cassel was ready. He swung his own gun, and the shock of steel against bone was a solid, almost sickening sound. The other man collapsed half on top of the first, who was striving ineffectually to get back into the fight.

Standing up, Cassel brought his gun-barrel down again, quieting both of them. It had been warm work while it lasted, but brief. Their own haste had ruined things for them, but he had counted on that, having seen it happen times enough before.

For a space of seconds he stood unmoving, gun in hand, back to the wall of the office, waiting, listening. But there was no other sound, nothing at all save the throbbing of his own head, as though a sledge-hammer beat there on a rusty anvil. Convinced that these two had been alone, he closed the door again, and the added darkness was like a heavy weight. Holstering his gun, he scratched a match, well aware that if he was making a mistake that this could be his last. But nothing happened, and he saw the lamp on Paddy's desk, crossed to it and blew the match out as it burned his fingers.

He lifted the chimney off, finding it still warm, set it down and lit a second match. Drawing the flame across the wick, he replaced the chimney with a little difficulty since one of the metal lugs which held it in place was bent inward, out of shape. Light drove out the blackness, and he saw then how thorough had been their search of this room already.

Evidently the two men had been here for some time. The room was in even greater disorder than the living quarters of Sime Kellogg, down below. Papers had been pulled out of desk drawers, searched hastily and dumped in a heap in the middle of the floor. The safe which had stood against a wall had been opened, showing that at least one of these men had had experience with such jobs before. The door stood open, the contents scattered about.

Nor was that all. The heavy rug on the floor had been jerked up, as though it might hide something. If there was anything which had not yet been looked into, the room gave no evidence of it.

But the pair had still been searching when he came, and neither of them had anything in their pockets now, as he made sure. Which seemed to argue that, whatever had been the object of their search, they had not discovered it.

Cassel could hazard a pretty good guess as to what it was. These men, it was a hundred to one bet, were from Horseshoe. Paddy had been just about to tell him where something was hidden, when that bullet from the darkness had sealed his lips, apparently for all time. Some secret paper or papers of whose existence Yoder was aware, and that secret had undoubtedly been Paddy's hold over him, a means of keeping him in line, enforcing truce.

If those papers should turn up, they might well hold ruin for Yoder within them. But he was risking that now, playing a bold game for full control of Bitter Creek, but leaving no stone unturned in the effort to get hold of them before anyone else could do so. Which argued that he was reasonably certain that no one but Paddy knew the secret.

And that was a secret which probably concerned Tincup and himself. Paddy had been about to tell him where the papers were hidden, but first he had exacted a promise that it would not be used while he was alive and able to make use of it himself.

If there was a game of double-cross here, in which he had been whip-sawed between Paddy and Yoder, there was nothing surprising in that, either. Paddy, more especially when a man was away to the wars and not too likely to return, would have no scruples there. Cassel's return might have changed his mind, but more likely it had only forced his hand.

Yet if this guess was so, it was as important for him, now, to find those secret papers first, as for Yoder to do so.

Yoder had apparently been convinced that

they would be here in Paddy's office, had sent these men to get them. A better watch would have to be kept on the store from now on. Kellogg wasn't much of a watchdog.

The two were beginning to stir now, to revive a little. He found a length of cord on the floor, where it had been tossed in the general confusion, there was a pair of shears in a half-opened drawer of the desk. Slicing off a couple of lengths, Cassel worked expertly, and had their hands tied before they had recovered enough to object.

One of them cursed, then, as realisation came to him, gazed at Cassel in dismay. He was a little man, a head short of six feet, sandy haired, wiry, an old scar twisting across his left cheek and to the corner of his mouth, like a livid, full-blooded angleworm.

'What's your name?' Cassel asked, and was rewarded with a scowl.

'Don't worry, I'll find out,' he promised, and picked up the extra dropped gun. Holding his own, he hesitated, then, using the remainder of the rope, tied the two together, a few feet apart.

'March,' he ordered. 'And one trick puts you in Boot Hill in the morning.'

The warning was sufficient. They walked docilely down the stairs and toward the rooms at the rear of the big store. A light shone from them now, and Kellogg's voice, a little frightened, came back as Cassel called out to him to open the door.

'I'll shoot to kill,' Kellogg warned. 'Don't think I won't, this time.'

'This is Cassel,' Cassel repeated impatiently. 'I've got both of them tied up. Open the door.'

There was a moment of hesitation, then Kellogg did so, holding a big revolver in one hand, still looking a little dazed and uncertain. Relief washed across his face as he took in the situation.

'Did—did you get the two of them, alone?' he asked, incredulously.

'They're here,' Cassel said shortly. He caught a glimpse of himself in a mirror which hung, badly askew, and blinked in disbelief. His wound had about stopped bleeding, but his head and beard were bedabbed with drying blood, and he looked fearsome enough.

'Who are these fellows?' he asked. 'I suppose you know them?'

Kellogg nodded.

'Sure do,' he agreed. 'The little fellow's Weidmier, and that's Post. They're Horseshoe hands.'

'I figured as much. They were tryin' to find somethin' in Paddy's office, upstairs. You any idea what?'

Kellogg shook his head.

'I wouldn't know,' he said. 'All I know is this store. I was hired to run it. Paddy didn't tell me about his private business.'

'Maybe you fellows would like to talk,' Cassel suggested.

'And maybe we wouldn't,' Weidmier snarled. 'Best thing you can do, mister, is to let us go—pronto. And then make tracks out of this country before daylight. You can't buck Horseshoe.'

'Maybe you'll change your tune before we're through,' Cassel shrugged. 'I'll take you over and lock you up. Kellogg, you'd better get some of Paddy's gun-guards and have them keep an eye on this place from now on. Just in case.'

'I'll sure do that,' Kellogg agreed, with an uneasy glance around the dim spaces of the store. 'Right away.'

'And I came over here to get some white cloth,' Cassel added, remembering. 'Miss Kenney wanted it. Could you get that for me?'

'Sure,' Kellogg agreed. He looked at Cassel, and filled a basin with water from a tin bucket.

'You better wash up a little 'fore you take anything back there,' he suggested. 'You look a fright. I'll keep an eye on that pair.'

Cassel accepted the suggestion, then ran a comb through his hair and beard. The cut, from the glancing blow of the gun-barrel, was not a bad one, and the cold water on his face refreshed him considerably. With the cloth wrapped and draped across his shoulder, and one of Paddy's men, whom Kellogg had summoned, to aid him, he herded his still sullen captives to the little, long-unused jail, and inside. It was substantially built and would hold them well enough, unless an attempt was made to free them, as they plainly believed would be the case. Privately, Cassel doubted it.

He returned to the *Cattleman*, and as he entered, came face to face with Yoder, who had just come down the stairs. Yoder's eyes narrowed at sight of the cut on his head.

'I got this from one of your crew,' Cassel said without preamble. 'Post and Weidmier were going through Paddy's office. I've got them in jail now. Are you backin' them in that, Yoder?'

Yoder looked startled for just an instant. Then his mouth tightened.

'The only men I ever back,' he said, 'are winners. If those two have been up to devilment and got caught at it, they'll get no help from me.'

CHAPTER ELEVEN

Having selected his place, a few miles out of Canyon, where the road narrowed sharply, running between a high steep bluff on one side and a crowding boulder, as big as a homestead's shack, on the other, Reynal made his preparations leisurely. He anticipated no trouble.

A scattering of trees, mostly scrub pine, grew back from the road, and chokeberries, the limbs laden with purpling fruit, grew beside the boulder, half hiding it. Just beyond, the road dipped sharply, so that the horses, pulling the stage, would have to labour to the top of the rise at a walk. It was a perfect place for his purpose.

Unhurriedly, Reynal dismounted, leaving his horse hidden in the brush and trees behind the boulder. He noted that his big boots made a clear pattern in the soft ground, and grinned. These were Dutton's boots, this time, and when their imprint was found, it would only add to the puzzlement of this one-armed marshal. He snorted disdainfully at the thought of a cripple trying to hold down such a job.

From a pocket he pulled a large blue bandana, in which he had already slit eye-holes, then, as he glimpsed the approaching stage, half a mile away, he slipped the mask over his face, made a final adjustment, and waited.

The stage had dipped out of sight now, though he could still hear the hollow rumble of its wheels and see a small haze of dust following in its wake, dissolving in the sunlight. He did not see it again until it was half-way up the steep pitch which led to his ambushment.

When it did come in sight, he received a shock. To-day there was not only the driver on the box, but the bulky figure of Mike Gerard, express guard, as well. Slouched there like a sleepy Buddha, with a sawed-off shotgun cradled in his arms.

The Fox had not counted on Gerard. It wasn't often that he was hired to make the trip, leaving a little cross-roads store which he ran down the Musselshell. When he did, that meant something of real value in the express box. And Gerard was not only a good shot, but a stubborn man.

His presence complicated things, but it had been so long since there had been a hold-up on this line that he wasn't very alert to-day. Reynal stepped out suddenly from the brush, his gun lined on them, a sinister figure with the mask across his face, and his voice was high and harsh.

'Pull up!' he ordered. 'Don't try a move, either of you! Now throw down that stuff!'

Taken by surprise, the two men on the box obeyed. Gerard half-made to raise the shotgun, but checked the motion before the menace of the gun which covered him. The driver, after a moment, leaned down a little, tugged and heaved at the express box, balancing it; then, with his foot, he shoved it over the side.

Reynal hid a grin. They figured that was what he wanted, and he didn't aim to touch it. He was no bandit! He shifted the gun in his hand a little as someone fumbled inside the door.

'Stay where you are!' he ordered. 'Anybody sticks his head out gets a mouthful of lead!' He gestured again. 'Toss that mail-sack down, too!'

The driver's face showed his amazement at this order. But after a moment he obeyed, and it thudded in the dirt almost at Reynal's feet. Cautiously he stooped and picked it up in one hand.

'All right!' he grated. 'And now you can get going! And don't try turnin' around—'

Quick to respond, the driver was kicking off his brake, yelling at his horses. They snorted, danced, started to surge ahead, and in that moment, slewing suddenly half around, Gerard fired both barrels of his sawed-off shotgun.

The range was short, the blast of the buckshot a terrible and devastating thing. Only one factor saved Reynal from instant death. He had been swinging the laden mail sack up to his shoulder, and it was more or less a shield in front of his face and chest. It took the brunt of those murderous loads of buckshot, but not all of them. A part went clear through, others went around the edges.

To Reynal, it seemed as though he was being driven down, torn to pieces by the shock. Only one bullet struck his face, slanting into his jaw through into his mouth, where it struck a tooth. But it seemed to him that a handful of those vicious cutting pellets had churned into his stomach, others were in his lungs so that he gasped and coughed, retching pain shook him and blackness was hitting him like a heavy fist, driving him down.

Even in that moment, his reaction was swift and instinctive. His aim had been centred warningly on Gerard, and now he triggered back, and saw a small round hole spring up in the express guard's forehead, where the skin had been tight and smooth before. Gerard wobbled crazily for a moment, then slumped and rolled, tumbling to the ground in a heap, while the stage raced on and out of sight.

Reynal did not see that. The blackness had him now. How long it held him in crushing grip he did not know, but it was probably only a few minutes. Then he stirred and sat up, crying out sharply with the pain which this occasioned, and sat staring, a little stupidly, at himself, and at the dead man huddled in the dust beyond, who, he knew, had killed him as well. Instinct told him that death would be only a matter of time, and not too much of that.

The pain inside him was a tearing thing, and it reminded Reynal of a scene he had witnessed years before—of a white weasel, its glossy coat dreadfully stained with its victim's blood, tearing the heart out of a big wild turkey cock while the turkey still gasped and quivered, and almost crawling inside the still living bird to do it. The same thing, he felt, was happening to him.

He stared at himself as his head cleared a little, incredulous. He had killed men before—several men, and it had never impressed him particularly. The incomprehensible thing was that this could happen to himself. He had never seriously considered such a possibility.

The blast of buckshot had knocked him down, unconscious. But now, with the first rending shock past, pain or nerves were numbing so that he hardly noticed it. He remembered the mail sack then, the thing for which he had risked all this, and Robert Yoder's injunction as to what he was to do.

Even in that moment, it never occurred to him not to finish the job he had started.

He puckered his lips to whistle to his cayuse, which always came at his call, and was surprised and a little disturbed when no sound came. Somehow the air was leaking out of him. Clutching the mail sack, leaning back against the boulder, he lifted, blenching anew with the pain, all but tumbling as his knees tried to buckle. By a supreme effort he stood up, clutching the edge of the big stone to steady himself.

He saw his revolver lying there at his feet, and regarded it with a detached interest. Up to now, it had been the most important thing he owned, useful and necessary as a hand. Now it no longer mattered.

Close by now he saw his horse, and moved to reach it. He staggered and fell against it, and leaned there for a few moments, too weak to move.

As he opened his eyes again and raised his head, he could feel the cayuse trembling, frightened of the smell of blood, of his condition. Yet, knowing him, and well-trained as it was, standing and waiting. And that, he realised dully, was his only salvation. For, stubbornly and unreasonably, he had decided that he wouldn't die, not this time.

It took three separate tries before he could drag himself into the saddle, and his hands were sticky with blood. The pain was coming back now, too, but he rode away, back through the scrub pines, as he had planned to do, still clinging to the mail sack, without quite realising what he was about.

He started suddenly, realising that he had been asleep, or almost unconscious. Something. His horse had stopped and was looking around at him inquiringly, and he knew that it realised that something was seriously amiss, and was troubled. He started to get down and slipped, and fell in a heap and the sack on top of him.

Shying away, his horse began presently to crop the grass not far off, troubled but uncertain. A faint sound came to him, and looking whence it came, he saw that Bitter Creek flowed there, not more than fifty feet away—clear and sparkling, and for the first time he became aware of the torment of thirst.

Now, sitting up, he remembered the mail sack and why he was here. Methodically, mechanically, he got it open, by reaching in where the buckshot had torn a gash. He pulled and slid the mail out on to the ground beside him in a little pile. The papers he gave only one glance. But there were half a hundred letters, and he had to stop and concentrate painfully before he could remember what letters were for, or what he was supposed to do with them.

But his head cleared a little then, and the pain, once again, had subsided to a sort of dull ache which seemed to encompass all of him. He observed, with a kind of surprise, that the grass where he sat was bloody, that some of the blood had made a dirty mud. But this seemed all apart from him now.

Some of the letters he could tell, just from the address, were of no interest to him, and he tossed them aside un-opened. Others were not so legible, or shot had ripped them and made them hard to read, or blood had smeared the envelope. These he tore open, with a slow earnestness, and pulled the contents out and looked at it enough to know that it was not what he wanted, before discarding them.

He was half through the pile when he found the letter he wanted, the one that Doc Gray had written. Why or what he wanted of it he couldn't remember, but he tore it across and across, and then sat staring stupidly, wondering if he had done the right thing.

As though his flow of strength had come from some hidden, unexpected reservoir, and had lasted only until he should have completed his job, weakness came back, in a dizzy wave, and pain and a rending nausea. He coughed rackingly, and it seemed to tear him in two, blood bubbled suddenly from between his lips.

Now he could no longer see the creek, for it seemed to be getting dark. The sun must have set, he decided, though it was funny that it should do so so early in the day. But he could no longer feel its warmth, either, so it must be so. Darkness was creeping in, stalking him.

But the creek was still off there. He could still hear the musical gurgle and splash of the water, and his thirst, by now, was a consuming thing. On hands and knees, crawling painfully, he started towards it.

Bitter Creek! That was what it was called, but its waters, he remembered, were very sweet and cold, and it would be nectar of the gods if he could reach it and stretch at full length now and drink his fill of it. Water!

His mind was playing him queer tricks, now. Or maybe he was dreaming. At all events, it was a pleasant dream. He was a little boy again, rosy-cheeked and eager, and going out to the well, working the windlass, allowing the old pail to drop with a sort of hollow splash into the deep, cold waters far below. Then, winding it up to the top, pausing to take a drink, tipping the water into another bucket, and carrying that across the yard and into the kitchen for his mother.

'You'll be a big man, some day,' she always said then. 'A fine man, I'm sure.'

Funny, he thought, in a moment of rationalism again. It had been years since he had remembered any of that—or his own sure certainty of what a big, fine man he would be—his mother's faith. For a long time he had deliberately schooled himself never to think, never to remember. Now it didn't seem to matter.

Water—and he could hear it, so close, so tantalisingly close. He had stopped crawling, but he tried it again now, dragging with his hands, and the dark was all about him. But that must be his mother, lighting a lamp in the window. A lamp for him to find his way home.

CHAPTER TWELVE

Paddy was awake, and in possession of his faculties. That was easy enough to see when Cassel visited him the next morning, even without Doc's word for it. He lay there, his eyes wide open, very bright, looking up at them, at Doc and Cassel and Quantrell, who had left his chair and come to stand in a wordless silence with them. For Paddy, it was as though the man had finally discovered, too late, that he had a soul. Now it looked at them from his eyes, and could tell nothing of the message he so desperately desired to impart.

'It's tragic,' Doc had warned Cassel simply, before they entered the room. 'Tragic, and amazing as well. By rights, he should be dead. But he's making an astonishing fight of it. Maybe he'll live—with nothing to live for.'

By which, Cassel knew, Doc was intimating that he could hold out no hope of recovery beyond life itself. Now, seeing the bright gleam in Paddy's eyes, after Doc Gray had gone out, Cassel told him what had happened—how his office had been ransacked by the pair from Horseshoe, and that they were now in jail. Quantrell had gone back to his chair, half-dozing.

'Whatever it was, Paddy, they didn't get anything,' Cassel assured him, and Paddy blinked a couple of times, rapidly. It was a strange sensation, talking to a man who could hear and understand, but could not answer. Cassel's face was sober as he left the room.

He would have liked to discuss various matters with Rusty, if he had been there. But Rusty kept the long night vigil, and Quantrell, with the odour of beer always on his breath, sitting there half-asleep, did not inspire conversation. It was lucky for Paddy, maybe, that he couldn't talk to him.

Kathleen met him in the hall outside.

'I've got good news for you,' she said. 'Anticlea's conscious this morning.'

'That's fine,' Cassel agreed. 'Doc seems to know what he's doing.'

'He's very good,' Kathleen said gravely. 'She's asleep now. But she asked about you when she was awake—and wanted to see you. Later, when she wakes up—'

'Of course, I'll stop in,' Cassel nodded. As he went out to breakfast, he wondered a little that she should want to see him. The meal finished, he turned into a barber shop. With that wound on his head, it would be easier to keep clean if he had it shortened, and now his beard, increasingly an aggravation, might as well go.

Half an hour later, looking at himself in the mirror, he was mildly surprised at the change. The long, lean jaw which the whiskers had hidden felt curiously smooth. He had made a clean sweep, hair trimmed, beard and moustache gone. It gave him a radically altered appearance, more like the man who had left Bitter Creek four years back. He looked ten years younger, and he smiled a little sardonically at the reflection. Maybe it was his whiskers which had affected Anticlea so strangely the other day. He remembered now that, up to then, she had never seen him with them on.

Back at the *Cattleman*, he saw the surprise in Kathleen's face, and knew suddenly that she believed that he had done this on account of Anticlea. And felt a vague irritation that she should think so. He hadn't been thinking of Anticlea at all in connection with the beard. It had simply been a matter of habit, having grown to profuse length during his long months in prison, when there had been no good means of shaving. Now it was off because it had been a nuisance.

He wanted to tell Kathleen so, but it was not a matter to explain, nor had he ever been a man to offer many explanations. He turned a little abruptly, and tramped up the stairs, and softened his step at Anticlea's room, as Mrs. Kenney met him at the door.

He saw the surprise in her face, as she looked at him, and the quick approval as well. Then she nodded for him to go on in, and slipped out and down the stairs.

As he had expected, Anticlea was awake, looking white and wan, but immeasurably better than before. She was almost lost in the big bed, propped among the pillows, and her eyes, doubly big in her pale face, were fixed on him as he crossed the room. In them he read more surprise and pleased approval, and she lifted one hand and gave it to him, letting her fingers remain in his.

'Clyde,' she breathed. 'Now you're my old Clyde again—and handsomer than ever!'

'You're a lot better looking yourself, this morning,' he said, and felt the words to be inane, but saw that they seemed to please her. 'We were afraid of how badly you might have been hurt, for a while.'

'The team ran away,' she explained with child-like directness. 'I guess it was my fault, too. Seeing you again—and that empty sleeve! I never knew—or guessed, Clyde. It—it hit me hard.'

That was true enough, he knew. Her reactions had been too genuine for any sort of acting, and his heart warmed to her a little at the realisation that she had not known of his hurt. But in the next breath he hardened again. She might at least have waited for his return, to see for herself.

'How did it happen, Clyde?' she asked, and her fingers, lying in his big hand, squeezed it a little.

He didn't want to talk about it, but the memory that she was still very sick stopped him, for she must be humoured a little. His voice was emotionless as he explained.

'A cannon-ball shattered it above the elbow. There wasn't much choice in the matter.'

He saw the horror in her face as she pictured that in her mind, and his own face tightened a little at the memory of it. What he had told her was not the truth, but it was as good a reason as any, and as close as he could ever tell her.

'I'm sorry,' Anticlea said, after a moment, and he saw the stark tragedy in her eyes again as she looked at him. 'You must hate me, Clyde, I've treated you very badly.'

'I don't hate you,' he denied, and knew it was the truth. The thing which surprised him was the almost utter absence of feeling in him, now that he was talking to her again. She was as beautiful as ever, even more so than he had remembered. But he seemed, in these last few days, to have been washed clean of all emotion. Love and hate had both lost their sharpness.

'You're very good to me, Clyde—but then, you always were.' There were tears sparkling in Anticlea's eyes, but she blinked them back, and as he tried, with sudden dismay, to withdraw his hand, she clung to it tighter. 'And the way I treated you—I've been such a fool—'

'Here, here,' Cassel protested, a little wildly, looking around desperately. 'You mustn't excite yourself, you know. Probably you've talked more than you should already—'

'Doctor Gray said I could talk to you as much as I wanted to. I'm all right,' Anticlea said, and her mouth was stubborn. 'I've just got to talk to you, Clyde.'

There was nothing else for it, apparently. His estimation of Doc Gray sank a little, and he tried one last tack.

'But you're a married woman, now—'

'That's just it!' Anticlea said fiercely. 'I'm a fool! Why I ever let him talk me into marrying him—oh, Clyde, if you'd just got back a little sooner!'

The tragedy was back in her eyes again. And, knowing Robert Yoder, the persuasive way he had when he wanted something, the persistency with which he worked to get his own way, Cassel could partly understand that. It was like rain, wearing away a hillside—washing a little here, a little there, under-mining, keeping at it until finally the whole bluff would collapse.

'I hate him!' Anticlea went on. 'Hate and despise him! If you only knew—'

Cassel stood up abruptly. He should have made allowance for her weakness, following such illness, for a mind not quite steady, and not have allowed this to happen. Hate her husband she might, even as he did—but the unalterable fact remained that Yoder was her husband, and to Cassel's mind there were no circumstances or set of them which justified him in listening to her talk in such a manner about the man she had married.

'I've got to be going,' he said, a little harshly, and turned at a sound to see Yoder standing in the doorway, a strange expression on his face—half of rage, half a mocking, fleering triumph.

Beyond him, out in the hallway, was Kathleen. And there was no doubt but what both of them had heard the last part of what Anticlea had said.

To Yoder, and perhaps to Kathleen as well, it must look as though he had suddenly jumped up in the guilty knowledge of being discovered. They could scarcely think otherwise. Kathleen was hurrying on down stairs, but he had to pass Yoder at the door.

Neither of them spoke. But that fleering look was stronger than ever in Yoder's eyes now, and behind it a cold, deadly rage which seemed to emanate from him like the heat rays from a red-hot stove on a cold morning. A rage to match that which was seething in Cassel himself.

CHAPTER THIRTEEN

The evidences of the hold-up were plain to read when Cassel arrived on the scene. Mike Gerard still lay where he had tumbled from his high seat, dead before he hit the ground. His empty shot-gun was near at hand, the left barrel bent and stove where it had struck sharply against a rock.

A passing rider had seen him lying there and, circling around, had hurriedly brought word to town.

The express box lay where it had been pitched from the boot, dusty but untouched. Cassel studied it with frowning eyes, for by rights it should have been the goal of any hold-up. But the trail of blood left by the lone stick-up man in his flight could offer the explanation.

Leaving the others who had accompanied him and still wished to, to take the body in to town or follow later, Cassel followed that blood trail, preferring to study it alone. It was plain, and not too far before he found Reynal himself, lying a scant yard from the edge of Bitter Creek. He had been crawling to the last, trying to reach the water, but on his face was a strange look of peace and contentment. His horse grazed close by, repelled by the scent of blood and death, yet held there by something stronger than its fear.

Here was the mail sack, its contents scattered. And the pile of letters which had been ripped open in the process, each with its stain of blood to attest to the grimness of that search. Which could only mean that the mail sack had been the real object of the robbery.

Patiently he searched through them, fitting letters back into the proper envelopes, replacing these in the mail bag. But one letter he studied with more than usual interest, reading it twice. It was evident that this had not been the object of Reynal's search, that he had given it but a passing glance before discarding it. This letter which, but for a pair of boots, now on the dead man's feet, would have gone on the previous day's stage.

To Cassel, the letter contained a lot of interesting features. It was Robert Yoder's handwriting, which he had seen often enough to recognize. It was addressed to Miss Rose LaVelle, at Dead Man's Creek—a town as unsavoury as its name. And the contents were particularly intriguing.

It would be easy to make a copy of the letter and send, keeping the original. There was not too much difference between his own handwriting and Yoder's. Rose LaVelle could hardly be expected to know the difference.

Cassel thrust the letter inside his coat pocket, and turned at a sound. He was a little absent-minded, supposing these men to be others out from town. Instead, he found himself staring into the levelled muzzles of two revolvers. Behind them, lounging in their saddles, were Baby-Face and Brager—Robert Yoder's two special gunmen, who had been with him when Cassel had first encountered him on his return to the Bitter Creek country.

The looks on their faces now, as well as the guns and the way they handled them, could not be mistaken.

'Raise that one hand o' your'n, Cassel,' ordered Brager, and his tone held a jovial quality which rang false.

'One dead man ought to be plenty in one place. Baby-Face, you take his hardware.'

Baby-Face, with a round, full face and unblinking eyes which were anything but baby-like, dismounted and helped himself to Cassel's gun, felt him over briefly for a hide-out weapon, and spoke squeakily.

'He's dehorned.'

'That being the case,' Brager nodded. 'Climb on your cayuse, Cassel. We're ridin' out of here.'

Cassel obeyed, watchfully. He had a pretty accurate idea of what this ride meant. They threaded their way deeper into the hills, heading gradually westward. The two rode a little way behind him, saying nothing, but holding on to their guns. Off at the side was Tincup, and sleek cattle, wearing the Horseshoe, looked indifferently at them as they passed.

They rounded a shoulder of hill, and were in a little, canyon-like valley, where the hills seemed to crowd from every side. Cottonwoods followed a small tributary of Bitter Creek where it hurried as though fearful that the illusion of closing hills would become reality and trap it short of the sea. Aspens clung to the sharply-rising slopes of a coulee, and their leaves were tinted with the bright yellow of the first frosts. A beautiful spot—but lonely, far removed from anywhere. And here, as he had been expecting, was Robert Yoder.

The boss of Horseshoe lounged on a springy cushion of grass, while his horse grazed with dragging reins a little way off. Stretched to full length, it was apparent that Yoder had tried to relax while he waited, and that anger and bitterness had run so strong in him that to take it easy had been out of the question. He had kicked holes in the ground with his heels, jerked savagely at the grass, had jumped up to stride back and forth before sitting down again.

Now, however, he came leisurely to his feet, his eyes fixed on Cassel with a slow vindictive triumph.

'Got him, I see, boys,' he murmured, and the words themselves held that undercurrent of stirring hate, rasping across the nerves like the warning whirr of a rattlesnake.

'Sure we got him,' Baby-Face nodded. 'What you want done with him now?'

'Just wait—for the present,' Yoder said, and Baby-Face flushed redly at the tone, but subsided. Yoder came a few steps closer to where Cassel looked down at him, almost indifferently.

'Cassel,' Yoder said, and his own tone was suddenly formal, almost precise. 'You should know that there are some things that I don't stand for.'

Cassel knew what he meant, knew that he was justified in his anger. But in the larger sense there could be no justification for this man in anything that he had done, considering his methods. It was all a masquerade with him, trying to simulate the righteous anger of a husband where even that anger was a cloak for the vileness in his soul.

'That's news,' Cassel retorted. 'I didn't think you drew the line anywhere, Yoder.'

He saw the flush creep redly up across Yoder's neck and seem to flame when it reached his hair, and he took a quick step forward, his voice had lost its icy calmness.

'Take care,' he warned, 'or I'll forget about giving you a chance, even.'

'Oh? Then you think that driving me out of the country would be better for you, in the long run, than murder?'

From the murderous glare in Yoder's eyes, he saw that he had hit it exactly. But Yoder controlled himself with an effort.

'We always did curry each other the wrong way, Cassel,' he said. 'We've done it ever since I can remember. And we've always wanted the same things. That's why I made up my mind, a long time ago, that this country wasn't big enough to hold both of us. I lived in hope, for a long time, that you wouldn't return.'

'Hope?' Cassel asked, mockingly. He leaned forward in the saddle, and at something in his face now, Yoder retreated a step, the two listening men clutched their guns with hands which were suddenly sweaty.

'Your wife asked me, when we talked, what had happened to my arm,' Cassel said thinly. 'I told her that it was shattered by a cannon-ball. That wasn't quite true, Yoder. What really happened was that a man with whom I'd campaigned for weeks, and slept in the same blankets with, shared my last crust of bread with—a man that I'd figured was my friend—when a good opportunity came, during a battle, shot at me at close range, to try and kill me.'

His eyes were blazing now, and Yoder retreated another step before the cold fury in them.

'He was a mighty poor shot. But he hit my arm. Then clubbed me over the head with his rifle as I fell. I looked up at him, and at the look in my face, he told me why he was doing it. Because he had been hired by you to find me and, when a good chance came, to kill me! He was to get a thousand dollars for it when I was dead!'

Yoder still shrank back. Cassel's laugh was tight and mirthless.

'And now you try to make me think that you boggle at murder! I drew my revolver with my other hand—I was always left-handed, remember?—and killed him before he could finish me. But gangrene took my arm!'

There was cold sweat on Yoder's face now, but he had control of himself again. He even contrived to smile.

'So that was what happened to him?' he asked. 'I'd often wondered. And you're a bigger fool than I took you for, Cassel. If you'd kept your mouth shut about that, I was intending to give you a choice. A chance to get out of this country alive, if you'd promise to stay out. For, when you give your word, a man can depend on it.'

'I'm giving you my word now, Yoder, that I'm going to kill you. I hadn't quite made up my mind whether you were worth it—but I guess it's a chore that has to be done.'

Red rage flared through Yoder's icy calm again.

'Why, you—you blasted, conceited—' he choked, and his hand half-dropped to his holstered gun, then he checked, shrugged.

'As I say, I aimed to give you that chance,' he finished. 'But you've sealed your own death-warrant. Take him, boys. You know what to do.'

He crossed to his horse, swung into the saddle, and rode down the canyon to where the hills seemed to bar the way, was swallowed suddenly and gone, not looking back. The other two had watched, their faces still a little pale, clutching their guns grimly, waiting in silence.

That was one last grand-stand play on Yoder's part. Cassel understood it well enough. He was always doing things in such a fashion. It would gratify his vanity, give him a sense of greater importance, to order a man's death rather than to do it himself. And he was completely confident that it would be executed.

Baby-Face's head swivelled around from watching his employer out of sight. His companion's regard, on the contrary, had never wavered from Cassel for an instant.

'Do we do it here, Brager?' he asked.

Brager shook his head.

'Farther back,' he said, and motioned with his gun. 'Get going, feller.'

There was no choice for Cassel but to obey. He knew that the revelations these two had overheard had shocked them, appalling as they were, and the fact that Yoder had not even attempted a denial had made it worse in their eyes. But they had known from the start that their mission was to take him back into some pre-selected spot in the hills and kill him, as Brager's words now confirmed. And, after the first moment of shock, they saw that there was no difference between the man who hired them, and themselves. They were all birds of a most craven feather.

So their resolution was unchanged in any way, as Yoder had known it would be. They had to kill him, now, and for them it had become more than a chore, but something personal as well.

Riding, with two cocked guns at his back, Cassel shivered a little. He had made that last brag to Yoder, knowing it to be such, but not able to resist the jab at the man's over-weening pride. Yoder had given him the perfect opportunity when he spoke of the worth of Cassel's word.

But there seemed little enough chance of living to ever carry that out, now. He'd been a double fool—not so much for telling Yoder that he knew the full extent of his treachery, as for hesitating about killing him, as soon as he had returned to the country. Since that day when Yoder had hired a man to hunt him out and kill him, the issue had been settled. He had known that at the time.

But that letter, from Anticlea, had changed things, made him indecisive. She had married Yoder, and for that reason he had let the thing slide, waiting for the course of events to make up his mind anew. That had been a mistake, and apparently a fatal one.

Here were chokecherries, their limbs heavy with purple fruit. Off at the side was a buffalo berry bush, and splashes of autumn colour rioted on every hand. They were pressing steadily deeper, back into the hills, into a wild tangle of country where even cattle never strayed. There was no good reason for any man to ride back in here, and few ever did. Back here, his bones could lie undiscovered and forgotten.

A sudden splash of rain struck him in the face. Cassel looked up, surprised. The sky had become overcast in the last couple of hours, but his mind had been far removed from weather. Now, as a fresh gust of wetness assailed him, sudden hope came back. He saw, looking around, that the other two liked it even less than he ordinarily would have, that it was going to hasten what they had to do. But it gave him a fighting chance, where none had existed before.

He looked back just in time to surprise a nod passing between them. Their guns had sagged a little as they rode, for escape, in here, was out of the question. But here was an open glade, not more than a stone's-throw across, with a tall pine tree standing sentinel at the far edge where rosebriars crept to border it, and a great fallen log, half-rotted, reaching nearly across it.

They were starting to raise their guns again, to aim and fire. But for just that instant they had looked at each other rather than at him, and the sudden gust of rain was stinging their faces. With the grim directness of a cavalry charge, Cassel swung his horse, and was between them, his own powerful beast plunging headlong to strike Brager's cayuse broadside and send it, screaming, back and down.

CHAPTER FOURTEEN

That was better luck than Cassel had expected. He had used such tactics in the heat of battle more than once, but usually a horse, if struck at all, would rear back and be only momentarily put out of action. Brager's cayuse had been too surprised to protect itself, however, and it was being bowled over, falling in a heap which sent Brager's shot high among the tree-tops.

Baby-Face was equally startled by this sudden show of resistance, where they had counted on it being a simple matter of seconds until his unconscious body would be riddled with their lead. He swivelled in his saddle, firing hastily, and missing. And by then, Cassel was out of the saddle on the far side away from him, and two plunging horses in between made it almost impossible to target him at all.

It seemed a scene of wild confusion, but Cassel knew precisely what he was doing. He had rehearsed such things as this before, in games full as deadly. He slipped around as Brager's horse come plungingly to its feet again, so that he had it for added shelter, and he saw that Brager, caught completely by surprise, had tumbled out of the saddle.

He hadn't been much hurt, if any. For now he was starting to scramble to his own feet. But the confusion of the thing was still upon him, and the gun he had clutched had tumbled out of his hand. It lay there in the new-wet grass, and Cassel scooped it up and swung, and saw Baby-Face, his horse now under control and the others out of the way, levelling his own gun to finish this.

Flame was making a red jab from the muzzle as Cassel shot from the hip, not bothering to bring the gun clear up. As he had reminded Yoder, it was his left hand which he had always used, and he saw the small round hole in the upper middle of Baby-Face's nose, slanting upward. The gun in Baby-Face's hand made a little arc as it fell from a hand gone limp, and then Baby-Face was tumbling out of the saddle as his cayuse twisted back in wild terror, was thudding into the grass there beside the big half-rotted log.

Cassel swivelled around, and saw that Brager, impelled by a wild terror, had succeeded in catching his own horse again, where it ran with dragging reins. He made a leap for the saddle, not stopping to use the stirrup, came into it on his stomach, lying across it, with the horse now running wildly. He was still clinging in that undignified position as the cayuse plunged out of sight in the brush beyond.

Thoughtfully, Cassel opened his coat, wiped the wet steel of the gun on the dry lining, then holstered it. It would have been easy to drop Brager before he was out of sight, but it seemed unnecessary. He'd keep right on riding, Cassel figured—clear out of Bitter Creek. And if he did that, he wouldn't stop to warn Robert Yoder that he had failed to do his job.

Baby-Face's horse was gone now as well. Baby-Face had ridden with the reins tied together, and they had caught over the saddle-horn, so unable to stop and graze, it would head back pretty directly for Horseshoe, and the empty saddle would be warning enough and a matter of speculation.

Cassel caught his own horse, swung to the saddle, and, holding the reins briefly under his knee, used his hand to turn up the collar of his coat. The rain was driving steadily now, and the gesture, he realised even as he made it, was a useless one. He'd be thoroughly soaked, long before he could reach shelter.

Abruptly, he swung his horse, almost in an opposite direction. That letter in his pocket, addressed to Miss Rose LaVelle, Dead Man's Creek, intrigued him. He was already well on his way toward this town of Dead Man's Creek, which was situated to the north, over across the Little Belts. A place with a reputation as unsavoury as its name . . .

'Might as well let Yoder enjoy himself with thinkin' I am dead, an extra day or so,' Cassel reflected, and stroked his smooth chin speculatively. 'Haman was hanged on his own gallows.'

He camped, when night found him, deep in the foothills of the Belts. It was still raining, but he found a sort of cave, back in a cluster of rocks, where he would be dry. The place was pungent with the odour of mountain rats who had found it a haven long since. But he had slept in plenty of worse places in the last four years.

The sky was clear, white frost carpeted the ground when he awoke. The chill had put an ache in his missing arm, and the stump throbbed convincingly. It would trouble him at such times, he knew now, to the day of his death. And that was another count for Yoder.

The air sharpened, despite the steely sunshine, as he rode higher, following now a long slanting slope, carpeted in brown, climbing again and twisting up timbered, sky-slashing slopes. Near the summit, a tracery of snow lay, fresh from the night. The outspread view was worth the climb. Far off to the southeast sprawled Tincup and Horseshoe. Beyond, barely visible even from the clear air, was Canyon, a tiny smudge of smoke blurring above it for identification. Between was unclaimed country, mile on mile of it.

North, and below, was another unclaimed empire. He found the stage road, twisting a tortuous way down heavily timbered slopes, with here and there a little stream brawling wildly, jumping down cliff sides and breaking itself, then subsiding into deep silent pools, only to break away again with untamed lustiness. Antelope crossed an open meadow ahead of him, their white flags bobbing rakishly. Cassel saw the cause at timber's edge, a ruff-necked grizzly, hungrily batting a rotten log to pieces, scooping up a wildly fleeing mouse or so.

Here was a lake, tiny, mountain-high, deep, with a moose rearing only his rump from out near the middle of it, then lifting antlered head for a snorting breath, before beginning his deep foraging again. Deer grazed at meadow's edge. A mile below, through a rift in the timber, he saw buffalo, a hundred head, fatly breakfasting.

'Everybody but me,' Cassel said,

half-sourly, and urged his horse to a faster pace. His appetite was uppermost in his mind when he came in sight of Dead Man's Creek, a little past noon. An unlovely example of how quickly man could spoil anything he touched, Cassel thought dourly, and sought a restaurant. And eating, despite his hunger, reflected on the meals that Kathleen Kenney cooked. And the thought of her was a warming thing, but with a quality of half-remembered sadness.

He studied the letter again, for what it might contain. It was a strange epistle, exactly the sort he would have expected Robert Yoder to write—a mixture of appeal and brazen instruction, of threat and promise. Of the arrogance that was in the man, overlording a touch of uncertainty which he seemed sometimes to feel. A familiar and insulting letter in its entirety.

In it, Robert Yoder reminded Rose LaVelle of a visit he had made, some weeks before, to Dead Man's Creek. And of the pleasant evening he had spent with her. He left it subtly in doubt whether it had been too much liquor or his own charm which had induced her to confide in him her reason for being in such a town and such a place in the town, but that she had given him her confidence seemed clear enough.

She had come west, it appeared, searching for trace of a long-lost brother, the darling of her mother's heart. That mother's failing health and desperate anxiety to hear from her son again was the reason. Apparently she had given the name that he had, at least in the old days, been known under. Some description of him had struck a chord in Yoder and convinced him that this was no idle tale in quest of sympathy and perhaps more whisky, but something which might hinge in truth.

That much Cassel could tell from what he read. Yoder had promised to keep an eye open for the stray. Now he was writing her to tell that he knew where her brother was, and that, for the price of her coming to Canyon, and coming in the guise of a nurse and as a respectable woman—which part he felt that she was qualified to play. If she would act as nurse to Anticlea until the time of Anticlea's death, he would see that her brother was restored to her.

There was more, in the same vein. A half-threatening, half-urgent letter, clumsily contrived and indiscreet, yet stopping just short of baldness. Cassel paid his bill, and mentioned the girl's name.

'Miss LaVelle? Yeah, she's in town, stranger. Runs that dress-makin' shop right across the street. Sure was a boon to the ladies, when she arrived in our midst. The way they're gettin' prettied up, us menfolks is going to have to start shavin', ever' Sat'day mornin', looks like, to hold our own.'

Cassel was a little surprised, for from the letter he had gathered that Rose LaVelle would be working in an entirely different sort of place. He was more puzzled when he had crossed the street, and entered the little shop. She was a tall girl, dark-haired, with eyes frank and direct and untroubled. And here, if he knew anything about it, was that respectability which Yoder had thought her capable of playing, but had just as evidently not considered her living up to.

'You wanted to see me?' she asked, and Cassel knew that he was right, that Yoder had been wrong. Likewise, voice as well as face, she reminded him of someone he had seen before, though he could not think who or where. Probably Yoder had noticed the same thing.

'I did want to,' Cassel conceded. He was suddenly aware of how travel-stained he was, his clothes having dried in the saddle, his fresh stubble of beard and all. But in a town like this, she was used to such things. He drew out the letter, handed it to her.

'This is for you, I believe,' he said. 'I'd like to have you read it, if you will—and allow me to explain.'

'Come in,' she said, making her decision, and she led him past the work-room where dresses and dress materials were strewn about in a disordered sort of neatness, and to a sitting-room beyond. Her eyes were questioning.

'My name is Cassel,' he told her. 'I am Marshal of Canyon. There was a stage hold-up, and the mail sack was opened, many letters opened as well. This was one of them. I read it—and it held more than ordinary interest for me. If you will read it, I'll explain that, too.'

With a murmur of excuse, she did so, and he watched the play of expression across her face—amusement and contempt and anger, interest and bewilderment and anger again. But her gaze was still frank when she looked at him again.

'Mr. Yoder was here about five or six weeks ago,' she said. 'I had just come to town, then. That evening, I had gone to a saloon to ask if anyone had ever heard of my brother. It seemed the best way to learn anything. I was there when he came in.' Her cheeks coloured faintly.

'He seemed to assume at once that I—that I was an inmate of the place. But I saw that he was known, and accorded a lot of respect, and he was from another town. So I allowed him to buy me some supper and several drinks, which I did not swallow—though he didn't notice that. If he got a wrong impression of me—that was his fault.'

'I was sure of it, when I saw you,' Cassel agreed gravely. 'That is the one thing which has always stopped him from being a great man—he is too big a fool in some ways.'

'Yes,' she agreed, and glanced at the letter again. 'He—he says that he knows where my brother is—that he is serving a life-sentence for murder, in a penitentiary in another state.' Her eyes sparkled. 'I don't believe it! And if that's so, how could he get him pardoned, if I did whatever it is that he wants?'

'I'm not sure,' Cassel said thoughtfully. 'But I have a notion that he's telling the truth in part—that he does know who your brother is. Though I don't think that he's behind bars. You can see, easily enough, what he wants.'

Rose knit her brows.

'It sounds as if he wanted me to nurse his wife—until her death! As though he expected me to give her the wrong medicine—or something.'

'I think that's precisely what he has in mind,' Cassel agreed. 'He thinks that you're in no position to refuse. And note what he says: "This letter will be your guarantee that I will keep faith with you." Sort of a club to hold over his head, in return for the club he thinks he has over you.'

'But it's monstrous!' Rose exclaimed. 'His own wife.'

'Are you surprised?' Cassel asked quietly.

She considered a moment, shook her head.

'No,' she confessed. 'Not much. And as

you say, for all his brains and ability, he has a wide streak of being a fool.' She looked at him keenly. 'This lady—Anticlea. She is something to you?'

'I was engaged to marry her, before she preferred Yoder to me,' Cassel nodded. 'That's all past. But as a law officer, and as an old friend as well, I naturally don't want to see her murdered.'

'Naturally not,' Rose agreed, a little drily. 'What did you want me to do?'

'I was hoping that you'd come and take the job. Let him continue to think what he does. I'll be sure, then, that Anticlea doesn't die, from an overdose of medicine—or the wrong one.'

Rose tapped the envelope against her teeth, big ones, gleamingly white. Then she nodded.

'You want to set a noose about his neck,' she said. 'And after what he's said in this—I'll be glad to help!' Her teeth clicked. 'Do you think he does know anything about my brother?'

'I think that we'll learn something,' Cassel said carefully.

She considered that a moment, soberly.

'He was always a little wild,' she agreed. 'And you're afraid that it may not be all talk on Yoder's part. At least, it will be worth knowing. Mother has passed away, since I left—very suddenly. For my part, I can stand the truth. I'll take the stage out in the morning.'

CHAPTER FIFTEEN

There was nothing to remain in Dead Man's Creek for. And much to do at Canyon. Half an hour later, following the road this time, and with a fresh horse, Cassel was in the saddle. He should reach town by midnight, late enough that no one would need know of his return until the following day. By then, he suspected Robert Yoder was due for a jolt.

The perfidy of the man did not surprise him. Already he had seen too many aspects of it for any revelation to shock. And it was not so surprising that Yoder had acted as he did, in writing that letter. With his turn of mind, he naturally viewed everyone else as being influenced by motives no higher than his own, and judging Rose LaVelle as he had, such a letter to such a person would entail no particular risk.

Besides that, if he really knew who her brother was and where he was, he probably had a powerful weapon which could be calculated to keep any talking tongue silent. Actually, the thing that had spoiled all this had been the hold-up, which he himself had ordered. And the added fact, self-evident, that Reynal had not been looking for this particular letter or concerned in it at all.

Rose LaVelle, Cassel knew, was doing this partly for herself and for what she might learn, and partly for him. She believed that he was still in love with Anticlea. A woman would jump to that conclusion quite naturally. He considered that angle of it, with a sort of mild surprise.

Up to a few days ago, when he had received that letter, announcing her determinaton to marry Yoder, he had been very sure, over the long years, that he was in love with her. It had been that, more than anything else, which had sustained him through some of the ordeals he had undergone. He had been planning to marry her.

It seemed strange now to think that he could have been mistaken. Maybe, if he had found her waiting, and eager, the Anticlea of his dreams, there would have been no change. There was no way of telling about that, now. For there now was all that had happened in between.

Perhaps he had been living in a dream, which had been only that, for a long while. Certain it was that Anticlea roused no particular emotion in him now, when he thought of her—beyond sorrow and pity. He still thought of her as a friend, and he was desperately sorry for the situation in which she found herself.

But when that was said, all was said. He had seen her revealed for what she was—pretty and eager, but selfish, shallow. Whatever reasons she might advance now, the fact remained that she had married Yoder in preference to himself. She had known at the time that Yoder was the big man in the Bitter Creek country, had believed that he was destined to be still bigger. She had seen what he had done to Tincup, to the old home there, and still had done that thing.

An idol with feet of clay.

That was all, he saw now, with bitter clarity. There was no real depth to her, nothing beyond a pretty surface. She had opened his eyes roughly, but opened them more fully than she might ever guess.

The dark came down as he rode, but he was used to forays by night. His cayuse, fresh to start with, was laggard now, but he took no notice of fatigue for himself, or for the miles, his mind occupied with its searching introspection. The moon must be coming up at last. He raised his head, and saw that he was closer to Canyon than he had thought, and that this was no reflection of moon or even sun. This was fire—a holocaust in the centre of the town.

Flames leaped high, writhing red arms reaching to the crimsoned sky above. A great pool of fire which seethed and bubbled and struggled to fling itself even higher, and fell back upon itself in a sort of helpless fury. The Mercantile.

A crowd was gathered, back at a respectful distance from the heat, and some of them, with shovels and buckets, were taking such precautions as were possible to see that the flames did not spread to any of the other buildings. But the fact that the Mercantile had been set apart from all others had saved the rest of the town. Yet there would be nothing at all saved of it.

It had been a great store, a sort of dream of Paddy's made real. Containing the material things of life, the necessities and some of the luxuries. Canyon would be the worse for its destruction.

A dead man lay huddled at the edge of the darkness. This was Post, one of the two men he had caught rifling Paddy's office. Apparently Yoder, despite his assurance that he had no further use for them, had turned them loose during Cassel's absence. Rusty, a smouldering anger in his eyes, stood nearby.

'I caught him at it,' he growled, and touched the butt of his own gun significantly. 'But I was too late. Though if Quantrell had been on the job, 'stead of guzzlin' beer—'

His voice trailed into silence, still impotent with fury. The Merc, in Rusty's eyes, was Paddy, and this was another hurt to a helpless man.

'How'd it happen?' Cassel asked. 'Didn't

anybody see it in time to try savin' it?'

Rusty had moved on. The man who answered the question did not know Cassel in the dusk, nor recognize him. His answer was blunt.

'Mister,' he said, 'when we first saw that fire, it was sweepin' the buildin' from end to end. You might as well spit against hell!'

So that was it! Not only had the fire been set, but probably in a dozen places at once. Unable to find those incriminating papers which Paddy kept hidden somewhere, Yoder had been grimly determined that no one else should ever find them, either. And he had already, long since, disclaimed all responsibility for the tool he had used!

★   ★   ★

Cassel had been mistaken in his estimate of Brager and what the gunman would do, though it was partly chance which turned the scale. Brager, following the killing of Baby-Face and his own near escape from the same fate, had been fully determined to do exactly as Cassel had expected him to—to keep travelling without a stop, to get out of the Bitter Creek country with all possible speed. As far out as possible.

The very thought of reporting to Robert Yoder was like a nightmare. But, by the time he had ridden for a while, and his already tired horse had settled to a slogging walk, a change came over him. With the steady driving rain soaking him and cooling him, his mind was beginning to function again, the shock of terror washed away. And it was then that he saw Baby-Face's riderless cayuse close at hand.

It too had raced for a while, with terror spurring it along, and the fact that the reins were tied together and looped over the saddle-horn had kept it going farther and faster than would ordinarily have been the case. But now it had run off that first fear, and was subdued enough. The thing was that it had headed for home in a straight line, and Brager had followed a somewhat longer trail, so that thick brush would not slap him in the face as he rode.

Brager eyed the horse in momentary surprise. Then, and without trouble, he caught it. An extra mount would be helpful in getting out of the country. Besides, it would compensate in part for the wages he had coming, his clothes and other things left behind at Horseshoe. Not to mention the five hundred dollars he was to have received as his share for the killing of Cassel.

Thought of that money touched him rawly, and then he got the idea. Now that he had Baby-Face's horse, there was no need of ignominious flight. The plan flowered swiftly in his mind, once germinated. He could tie this extra horse out in some coulee, well-hidden by the night and storm. Then explain that Baby-Face had ridden on into town.

And add that Cassel was dead, the chore done according to instructions. It would be simple enough. Yoder would be home, on Horseshoe, to-night. Cassel, whatever he did, wouldn't be likely to come there. Yoder couldn't possibly hear that he was alive until some time the next day. He would have no reason to doubt Brager's story.

He'd report the job as done. And add that he wanted the thousand dollars now, and was taking Baby-Face's share on into town for him. After such a job, Yoder would understand. With that money, and his duffel-bag, he'd get the extra horse, and be well out of the country by the time Yoder learned the truth.

And he needed that money. Likewise, he felt as if he'd earned it, with what he'd gone through. Brager had no compunctions as he turned in at Horsehoe again, for what he felt was the last time.

It was simple enough. Yoder paid the money without question, and presently Brager was riding again, but this time more comfortably, and with a slicker to cover him. The fact that it was Judd's slicker didn't trouble him. Everything was going perfectly.

By the next day, he was well beyond

danger, as he figured it, though he intended to travel for at least a week before he made a stop longer than overnight. Right now, he craved a change of scenery.

He heard the cattle that afternoon, before he sighted them, but thought nothing of it. Cattle were scattered widely in this country. There were a lot of small stray bunches through the hills, in addition to those which bore regular brands. Horseshoe predominating among them.

Too late, he came out upon the little herd of about a hundred head, with Judd and two other punchers from the ranch tagging after them.

Brager thought quickly. His first panicky impulse was to swing his horse and duck back for cover, but it was too late for that. Or to ride like the devil, but that would be sure betrayal and they would catch him sooner or later. The thing to do was merely to act as if this was what he had expected—as if he had come looking for them. That was it. Go on with them for a while. He'd be able to slip away, come dark.

But Judd's greeting was a little disconcerting.

'What the devil you wearin' my raincoat for?'

Brager shrugged, his face under control.

'Why shouldn't I?' he demanded. 'It was rainin' pitchforks when I started, and I couldn't find mine. I didn't think you'd care.'

'Sure you couldn't find yours, never havin' had one,' Judd flared. This whole expedition, to bring back a small bunch of stock, had grated on nerves already raw. There was no good reason why he, as foreman, should be sent off on a hand's job, unless it was to get him out of the way. And why should Yoder want to do that?

Whatever the reason, he felt that there was one, and it had increased his fury as the eternal slow drag wore on. He never had liked Brager, a feeling originally born out of jealousy, since Yoder had always picked Brager and Baby-Face for special jobs. Here was the chance to take some of his spleen out.

'What you here for, anyway?' he demanded.

'Why, I—I just came out to meet you,' Brager explained. 'The boss sent me. Figured you might need some extra help.'

'Extra help? With three men to a hundred head?' Judd looked at him in amazement. 'Are you crazy?'

'I mean, he wants you to get back, right away,' Brager added desperately. 'I was to take yore place.'

That was better, Judd reflected. Maybe they'd find out that he was the one who ran things around Horseshoe, after all. And then his suspicions centred again. Brager looked mighty uneasy, for some reason or other, and he was contradicting himself as fast as he talked.

'What you got two horses for, and yore duffel-bag packed?' he demanded. 'Looks to me like you was gettin' out of the country.'

Brager realized, with new panic, that he was caught. He'd forgotten that war bag, tied on the other saddle. Lying was getting him nowhere. The truth—or a discreet part of it—might work better. He smiled, a rather sickly leer.

'You're right, Judd,' he agreed. 'I am gettin' out. Drew my pay and pulled stakes. I've had enough. Here's your coat. So long.'

Judd accepted the slicker which he tossed at him, but his face did not relent.

'And so now you're quittin' and pullin' out, eh?' he asked. 'That sounds like the truth. But stealin' my slicker makes you a thief. And since when did Yoder give you an extra horse? You came in without a string, and you ride out with two.'

'A man needs a string,' Brager defended himself. 'I had wages, and I bought an extra horse.'

That was plausible enough. But his haste to be gone, his patent nervousness, had fully roused Judd's suspicions by now.

'Mebby you're tellin' the truth,' he agreed. 'Mebby not. You said first that you'd come out to help us. So you can. You can come right along back with us, and we'll check up.

If you're tellin' the truth, fine. If you're pullin' some shenanigan, that'll be somethin' else.'

Panic gripped Brager. Now he was in for it. If he was taken back to Horseshoe, where Yoder would by then have certainly learned the truth, that Cassel was alive and vengeful—the very thought filled him with an unreasoning terror.

'You can't make me go back,' he snarled. 'I've quit, I tell you. And a man's got a right to ride where he pleases.'

Judd gave him a slow look, and before that look Brager quailed. He was a gunman, a hired killer. But there was something about Judd which had made him foreman of Horseshoe, and it was a quality which terrified Brager almost as much as the thought of meeting Yoder again.

'You've yapped plenty,' Judd warned. 'Are you comin' without a fuss, or do I have to tie you?'

★   ★   ★

It was the next afternoon when the slow-moving herd reached Horseshoe, and Yoder himself was on hand to greet them. His face lighted at sight of Brager, but it was an unpleasant light which chilled the marrow of the gunman's bones.

'So you brought him back?' Yoder nodded.

'I'm sure glad of that, Judd.'

'Reckoned he'd been up to some devilment,' Judd said. 'Guess I made a good guess, eh?'

'You sure did,' Yoder was beginning, when Brager, with desperate eagerness, jerked out the thousand dollars and almost thrust it at his former employer.

'I thought he was dead,' he squalled. 'I sure did. Here's the money you give me—'

Yoder's looked checked him. It was a blend of coldness which froze him as ice could not have done.

'You can keep the money,' Yoder said softly. 'It's for killing a man. And he's back in this country. Judd, see that he's watched—all the time. He's not to leave Bitter Creek till he finishes the job he's been paid for.'

He swung on Brager again.

'*You've taken the pay for killing Cassel—and you'll earn it by doing just that—or I'll skin you alive!*'

CHAPTER SIXTEEN

Cassel slept late, following his jaunt to Dead Man's Creek and the fire on his return. It was past noon when he awoke, and he lay a while, looking up at the flowering roses on the wallpaper, where they made a gaudy riot along the wall and climbed to the ceiling. He was a little amazed at himself for sleeping so long, but he revelled in the feeling of luxury, of laziness.

It had been years since such a privilege had been his. Even in prison there had been no let-down, only a grey monotony of days, each a little worse than the preceding one. And since then it had been the same. Now, with everything gone that he had ever hoped or worked for, it suddenly seemed less important, and the right to rest after a long jaunt in the saddle was a thing of transcendent value.

He shook his head, smiling a little bleakly, and stirred himself, shaving. It was a chore that he had almost forgotten how to do, and took some time. Hunger was a sharp sauce in his stomach as he went downstairs.

He had planned to go out to a restaurant, but Kathleen met him, the blending odours of hot biscuits, steak and gravy and apple pie coming out of the kitchen with her. Her cheeks were flushed from bending over a hot stove, her eyes held some of the reflected warmth.

'Dinner's ready,' she said. 'And don't tell me that you didn't want to cause any extra trouble. You didn't. I haven't had my own yet. So come on and keep me company.'

Cassel did so, with a warm sense of

gratitude. He guessed that she had delayed her own meal, hearing him stirring around, but he could not complain. This was the sort of thing that he had dreamed of coming home to—he flushed a little with sudden self-consciousness and glanced at his empty sleeve. A man who had left part of himself behind on the battlefield had no right to dream dreams.

Nor had he done so for a long time. It had been his firm resolve to tell Anticlea that he was not the same man who had gone away, and to free her of her promise when he saw her again. But that, he reflected with sudden grimness, was a chore he had been spared.

Kathleen saw the old look of harshness come into his face, and was silent, pouring him a fresh cup of coffee, making no effort to intrude on his memories, and presently his face relaxed again. He stood up, almost regretfully, and looked around the room more fully than he had ever done before. There was a violin in its opened case, and he looked at Kathleen with sharp attentiveness.

'Do you play?' he asked.

She smiled and shook her head.

'No,' she said. 'I wish I did. Mother loves it—so do I. It was my brother's.'

And her brother, Cassel remembered, had gone off to die in place of Robert Yoder. He picked the fiddle up, gently, and held it a moment, and from the look in his eyes, the way he held it, Kathleen knew that he, too, had played—that his fingers throbbed now with longing to bring out the silent music here. He sighed a little, and put it down, but this time there was no bitterness, only regret.

'Kathleen,' he said. 'I take back one thing I thought. There are still more than two verities—and not all of them are harsh.' Not bothering to explain what he meant, he went out into the lobby, and after a minute, she heard him climbing the stairs again. And now he knew an odd regret, not quite tangible in his own mind, for that empty sleeve. It was, he supposed, the lack of a hand to hold the bow.

Paddy was awake, as usual. His eyes, which seemed the only part of him still alive, shone a little more brightly at sight of Cassel. It was as though he would use them to talk with, when hands and tongue failed him. Yet only a woman could say much with her eyes, Cassel reflected.

But if Paddy could talk—the idea struck him, and he considered it. Quantrell lounged back in his chair, tipped against the wall, looking half asleep as usual. Cassel would rather have been alone, but Paddy had had a gun-guard near or with him for years now, and Quantrell or Rusty was like his shadow.

Considering the thought, Cassel resolved on a bold stroke, knowing that the news of the fire had been carefully kept from Paddy.

Yet it was not the sort of news to get a man like Paddy down, great as was the loss.

'Yoder's still at it, Paddy,' he said. 'He aims to finish you—and me. The Mercantile was burned to the ground.'

If only that face of Paddy's was expressive, as it had been in the old days. Now it was more than the face of a poker player—it was a still face which told nothing at all. Almost the face of a dead man.

Except for the eyes. Paddy blinked, once. A look of excitement came into his eyes at the news, and he seemed to be listening avidly.

'It was burnt to the ground,' Cassel repeated. 'And by Horseshoe men. Rusty killed one of them—Post. My guess is that Yoder thought you had something hidden in your office that he wanted destroyed.'

He could not be sure but there seemed to be a momentary glint almost of triumph in those eyes now.

Sudden excitement gripped Cassel. He steadied his voice to a casual note.

'Paddy,' he said. 'You were starting to tell me something, when you were shot. I found the man who fired that shot. He's dead now. He held up the stage, and killed Mike Gerard. But Mike put a charge of buckshot in him to pay for it.'

While he was speaking, he was getting his thoughts in order. Once, as a boy, he had played a guessing game. Questions were asked, to be answered with a plain yes or no. Maybe it could be worked here.

'Your eyes are as good as ever, aren't they, Paddy?' he asked. 'Can you blink them for "yes"?'

The eyes blinked shut rapidly, opened again. There was no other change in the face—no vestige of a smile. The mask it seemed to wear now was like a mockery, but Paddy understood.

'If I ask you some questions, you can answer that way,' Cassel suggested. 'If the answer is no, don't blink at all. If it's yes, blink once. Is that clear?'

Paddy blinked again. It almost seemed as if there was a faint smile on his face this time, or at least about the eyes—as though he was trying, desperately, to force palsied muscles to act again.

'That's fine,' Cassel said encouragingly. 'Take it easy, and we'll lick this yet, Paddy. My guess is that Yoder figured you aimed to tell me about where you had hidden some papers that he didn't want to come to light again. So he had you shot, to try and stop you from telling. Then your office was searched, but they didn't find what they were after. So, if he couldn't get what he wanted, he intended to stop anybody else from doing it, either. And burnt the Merc, figuring that would do it. But it's my guess that those papers *never were in the Merc at all*! Am I right?'

Paddy blinked, twice. Cassel's face relaxed in a grin—almost the first time he had smiled since coming to Bitter Creek.

'I thought so,' he said. 'And you'd like to tell me where to find them, wouldn't you?'

Paddy blinked again.

'I think we can work that out,' Cassel nodded. 'We will start in a big way first. Are they in town, or in the country? If they're in town, say yes.'

Paddy stared, unblinkingly. Elation surged in Cassel. He had suspected that they wouldn't be hidden in town. But that left a vast amount of country in which they still might be cached.

'Are they in any other town?' he asked.

Paddy did not blink.

'Are they on Horseshoe?' Cassel persisted.

No sign. He tried again.

'On Tincup?'

Still Paddy did not blink. He was staring straight ahead, at the opposite wall—and not even looking at Cassel. Then, looking where he stared, a tingling excitement mounted in Cassel.

There was a shelf on the wall there, and a few odds and ends had been put there—a bottle, a small box which probably contained pills of some sort. But Paddy was looking straight at a tin cup.

Tincup! Paddy was giving him his answer.

And now, after a brief sidewise glance at Cassel, he closed his eyes, as though tired. Which he probably was. It wouldn't do to overdo, this first time. He could ask more questions later.

'Thanks, Paddy,' he said, keeping his voice even. 'Take a good nap now, if you can. We'll talk again some other time.'

But he had learned a lot. Those papers, which were so vital, had not been destroyed. And they were hidden somewhere on Tincup.

That took in a lot of territory. But it was a big step forward. Maybe to-morrow, when Paddy was rested, he could learn more.

* * *

Robert Yoder rode with a tight check rein on himself. He was conscious of rage which boiled and seethed within him, which, like steam in a tea-kettle, was constantly trying to lift the lid off with a bang, and it was not an easy matter to hold himself in. Yet now, he knew, it was vitally necessary to keep a sharp control of himself, if he was to be able to handle the situation which had arisen.

The thing puzzled him as much as it chafed. Everything had been going along nicely until the return of Cassel. It had seemed inconceivable to Yoder, from the eminence to which he had climbed, with ruthless arrogance, over the years, that a one-armed man, a beggar now in almost literal truth, could any longer shake him or even be a menace.

Once he had hired a man who was going off to the wars, to hunt Cassel down and murder him, and for a long time he had wondered whether or not he had succeeded. But when he had learned of failure, in that Cassel was alive and returning to Bitter Creek, he had not cared greatly. He was too big now, Cassel too small, to matter any longer. All that Cassel had ever claimed was now his own—Tincup, Anticlea. Yoder bunched them together in his own mind, with Tincup first.

Yet, in only a few days, the situation had changed. Again Cassel had demonstrated his luck, avoiding death as he had done before. The thing was baffling, almost frightening. What was far worse, he had all at once become a menace again, a greater threat to Yoder's security than at any time in the past.

And to top all that, he had succeeded in putting Yoder completely in the wrong, and himself on the side of the law—such law as there was. Now it had become a question of survival, and like it or not, Yoder knew that he must fight with any weapon at his command, with public opinion running strong against him.

It was that realization which forced him to order the burning of the Mercantile. Never in his life had Yoder hated anything as he hated that. The Merc, to him, meant more than it ever could to Paddy. It was the essence of his boyhood dreams, of that never-never land which kept receding like a mirage as he approached.

Because it was vitally necessary that Paddy's secret papers be destroyed, he had given the order. But the fire seemed almost to have consumed a part of himself. Its ashes were in his mouth. A rankling bitterness represented by Cassel.

But by taking such ruthless action, he figured, it would still be possible to eliminate Cassel. To grab firm hold on victory and dominate the valley again by force. But it was not so easy as he had counted on, and much was upsetting.

Such as the return of Brager, brought back by Judd. He scowled at memory of Judd. It was a good piece of work that the foreman had done, he conceded grudgingly; bringing Brager back, after the trick he had played. Likewise in getting back himself with those cattle, so speedily.

But that was exactly what Yoder had not wanted. He had sent him on that errand, figuring that he would consume at least three or four more days in the doing of it. Judd had explained his speedy return by saying that he had met the man who had sold Yoder the herd coming with them. The fool wanted to curry favour, of course, and had reasoned that he would please Yoder by doing that. Yoder ground his teeth. He'd like to shoot the man!

For Judd was back, and he couldn't very well send him off again. He had no good excuse, and Judd wouldn't take kindly to being errand-boy again. That was just one more example of how his plans had gone astray lately, despite the most careful calculation.

The thing which aggravated him above all else was the drastic course that Cassel was forcing him to adopt. Having become the biggest man in Bitter Creek, it had been his sincere desire to settle down as sort of a benevolent overlord of the valley, ruling with an iron hand where necessary, but keeping it encased in a velvet glove. To be done with violence and all that it implied, a man liked and respected more than he was feared.

That, too, was impossible for the present. It was a struggle now on primitive level, tooth and claw and no holds barred. Maybe it was just as well that Judd was back. Judd could be depended on for such a job as was ahead—

And if he worked it right, he could still contrive to keep Judd and Rose LaVelle from meeting, if she arrived. Maybe she wouldn't come at all. She should have been here two or three days ago, if she was coming, and there had been no word or sign of her.

Then Yoder spurred suddenly, as he came into town. The stage was just pulling in. And getting off it was Rose LaVelle.

And, as ill-luck would have it, Judd himself was standing not a stone's-throw away!

CHAPTER SEVENTEEN

From the look on the faces of the two, Yoder knew that he had not been mistaken in his own deductions. Judd was Rose's brother. He was crossing the street to her, amazement written large on his face, and Yoder cursed under his breath and tried to think fast. Luck seemed to have played him a dirty trick. And now, if ever he had, he needed a good story in a hurry, and had no least idea, where he could find one that would convince either of them.

That did not prevent him from infusing heartiness into his voice as he swung down from his horse and advanced, holding out his hand.

'Well, well, Rose, I see that I was right,' he declared. 'Not much doubt but what Judd here is your long-lost brother, eh? I wanted to play a little joke on you, in that letter—making out that he was enjoying free board somewhere. Though after the way you told me he'd been actin' I guess that's the way he deserves to be treated.'

The words came smoothly, surprising even himself with their convincing ring. Judd looked at him in amazement, a little uncertain, and Rose turned from Judd to accept his handshake.

'You seem to have found him, all right,' she conceded. *And now I know that you're a liar!* she thought, remembering the letter, and what Cassel had told her. She felt a surge of dislike for the man, but hid it. Cassel had urged her to come here to prevent what Yoder wanted done, and she was not yet quite sure how best to act.

Yoder decided it for her. He intended to keep firm control of this situation, now that he seemed to have it.

'Let's all go where we can talk, by ourselves,' he said, and led the way to the *Palace* and a room, talking steadily as they went. 'Quite a surprise, eh, Judd?' he asked jovially.

'Sure took me off my feet,' Judd conceded, staring at his sister as though he could not quite believe his eyes. 'You—you're sure grown up since I saw you, Rose,' he added. 'And—and everything.'

'You've changed, too,' Rose said, and found that she was neither shocked nor surprised by actualities. A few weeks in Dead Man's Creek, and the letter which Yoder had written her, had pretty well prepared her for the sort of man that Judd now so obviously was.

'Everybody changes,' Yoder said briskly. 'That's the way of life. I ran into your sister over in Dead Man's Creek, Judd, and she told me about you—how she had come west to try and find her brother. I wasn't sure then that it *was* you—since you never told me your last name. But I had a hunch, and I got busy and did some checkin'. I wanted to surprise you, so I kept still and wrote for her to come along.'

'That's true,' Rose admitted, realizing that the truth made only a thin veneer for a gross lie. Her grey eyes were level as she looked at Yoder now. 'But why did you want me to come and nurse your wife—until she died?'

She saw that the last phrase had jolted Judd. He looked with sharp suspicion at his employer, and Yoder coloured, but he had an answer ready.

'My wife has been injured,' he said. 'I need a capable nurse, and I thought of you. You misunderstood what I meant. What I meant to say, of course, was to nurse her as long as necessary—till she recovered, or—or died, as it looked then as if she would.'

Judd could sense a tension, and he didn't like it any better than the words. But he was still thinking of his sister and of home, of things long forgotten and suddenly recalled to mind.

'How—how's Ma, Rose?' he asked.

'Dead,' Rose said, with calm finality. 'She wanted to see you again, and I set out to try and find you. But it was too late.'

Judd's face grew stony, and in that moment, Rose handed him the letter. This was the one thing that Yoder had been dreading, and he tried to intercept it, and met Judd's sudden hostile gaze.

'What's the idea?' Judd growled. 'Mebby you better run along while we talk things over, Yoder. Been a long time since we've seen each other.'

It had been a long time, too, since anyone had talked that way to Yoder, especially a man who drew his pay. But he knew now that he had bungled this, and lost. That things had changed in the last few minutes, and would change more from now on. He managed a withdrawal gracefully enough, but the temper in him was mounting dangerously. He wouldn't be able to hold himself in much longer, he knew.

Judd looked at the door as it closed behind Yoder, a little uneasily, for old fealty was strong. And then he glanced at Rose, and saw the quizzical light in her eyes, and the open dislike for Yoder, and he read the letter. His brows drew together, and his breath came unsteadily, but he read in silence until he finished, then slammed it down on the table with sudden anger.

'I don't like this—any of it,' he flared. 'The way he writes to you—like you were a—a—'

'Apparently he judges everyone by himself,' Rose murmured. 'And the things he says about you—serving a lifetime in a penitentiary—'

'I've never served a day in my life,' Judd growled, and then, meeting his sister's gaze, his own eyes dropped. 'Not but what I've been pretty wild, I guess,' he added. 'But I ain't been in jail.'

He saw then that her gaze had shifted to the protruding butt of his revolver, where it stuck from the holster, to the neatly-filed notches in the metal braces of the heavy wood stock. His ears reddened.

'And I guess I would have been in jail,' he added heavily, 'if I hadn't got out of a couple of places when I did.'

'For killing a man?' Rose asked.

'Yeah.' His face was dogged now. 'Not that I ever figgered it that way. The first couple, they forced a fight on me. Figgered I was just a tenderfoot, and easy to push around. I had to do it, or be killed myself.'

The bluster and swagger was all gone from him, like an outworn coat discarded, and there was a sort of chill misery in his eyes now as he made confession.

'After that—well, it's like when you start a snow-ball rollin' down hill. You can't stop it. That give me kind of a reputation. Tough gunmen would come along, and want to build themselves up by fightin' somebody that was counted as pretty tough, too—and it just happened to be me. I didn't have no choice. But you see why I—why I never wrote—or came back.'

'I see,' Rose agreed. The thing would have shocked her terribly a couple of months before. Now it was not unexpected. This was a wild country, and Judd fitted into it perfectly.

'I don't know that I object too much to that, Judd,' she added, after a moment. 'I'll take your word for how it was. But do you have to work for a man like Yoder—and do the sort of work he seems to have to be done?'

'I been foreman of Horseshoe,' Judd said heavily. 'And that's been a good job.' He gazed blackly at the letter. 'Look like you had it figgered right—though why he'd want to kill his wife, is more'n I can figger—'

'The question,' Rose reminded him, 'is what you're going to do about it?'

Judd realized that only too well. He felt stifled, cramped, as if by the confines of the room, but it was bigger than that—bigger than he cared to admit to Rose. Sight of her, news of his mother's death, had shocked him, taken him back to boyhood, to that other, almost forgotten chapter of his life. Anger rose in him that Yoder would seek to use her for such a purpose, and a sharper, more bitter rancour that the man would deliberately plan to murder his own wife. For she was Anticlea.

He had always known his employer for a hard man. But even he had not guessed that Yoder could be a monster.

That anger was a cold and brittle thing, but it was countered by something else—by a sense of loyalty and responsibility to his job and the man who had paid him wages. And by something even more impelling—the fact that he had worked for Yoder because no other type of man would hire him. Yoder knew enough about him, if he so desired, to see him behind the bars of a penitentiary, or standing on a scaffold. And he had no delusions as to what Yoder would do if he turned against him.

Rose could understand something of his struggle, and she said no word, merely reached out and took the letter again. Judd watched her, and then he stood up.

'We'll take you over to the *Cattleman* an' get you a room,' he said. 'That's the best hotel. An' Yoder don't run it.'

He had little more to say while that was being done, but Rose knew that he had reached a decision. The formalities attended to, he turned away.

'You better stay here, Rose,' he suggested. 'It—it's a good place for a while. I'll see you later. Got somethin' to tend to, now.'

He went out, walking fast, as though forcing his legs to keep pace with what he had decided in his mind. His anger was still cold, but a sort of sardonic humour was building up along with it, a mockery directed against himself.

'What of it?' he jeered at himself, inwardly. 'What if Yoder does try to push you around? What you got to lose, except your neck—and that ought to've been stretched long ago, by rights. Here's one time you got to stand and fight it out—and for somethin' worth while, this time. When he tries to use your own sister that way, for murder—tries to murder his own wife—'

Judd's eyes were bleak at that recollection. Anticlea! He had never admitted it, even to himself, had never aspired to lift his eyes to the woman who was, even when he had first known her, supposed to be going to marry his boss. But Anticlea had meant something to him, and the thought of what Yoder had planned, the explanation of his callous acceptance of the news that she might be dying, roused a new bitterness in Judd now.

He strode on a little faster, then stopped suddenly. Here was a new angle that he hadn't even thought of, up to now. If he did this, then he'd be siding Cassel—riding along with the law. And Anticlea had once been engaged to Cassel! Judd laughed, deep in his throat, a harsh sound which held no humour.

Then he went on.

But Yoder, it developed, was no longer in town. It appeared that he had left rather suddenly, and Judd could guess why. His big shoulders hunched in resignation. Then he got his own horse, saddled it, and rode out of town as well.

He thought briefly of Rose, back there—of how he had promised to see her again, and might not. There was a lot he'd like to talk over with her, a lot of questions to ask her. And there was Anticlea.

But he dismissed them both from his mind and rode on. This was a parting of the ways, and what might happen at the forks of the trail was any man's guess, but one thing was certain. It wouldn't be pleasant.

CHAPTER EIGHTEEN

Restlessness was a strong current in Cassel, as he mulled over what he had learned from Paddy, and the necessity for waiting at least another day before he could question him again. Paddy had stared at that tin cup on the shelf, and then had closed his eyes as though tired, and gone to sleep. Probably he had questioned him too much for one time, as it was.

Tincup! The papers were hidden

somewhere on Tincup, but it was a big ranch, and that was not much of a clue. He'd have to narrow it down. In the meantime, he felt the need to be doing something, and yet there was so little to do.

In this spirit, he got his own horse and rode out, and it was partly a matter of old habit, partly a sort of hunger, partly the thing he had learned, incomplete as it was, that caused him to ride toward Tincup. There was bitterness that way, the reopening of old wounds, but he had to see it again, have a look around.

Not that he had any real hope of finding anything. But it was a good excuse for doing something. He came to what remained of the old buildings, the once-fine avenue of cottonwoods, and sat his horse for a while, looking at them. There were no cattle loitering here at the moment, everything seemed peaceful with the quiet of long neglect. It was like a tomb of lost hopes, but it drew him.

The rubble of the old milk house, tipped over and broken by trampling hoofs, the pile of foundation-stones, the mud of the spring it had covered, was like a slap in the face. He left his horse behind the old barn, and started for the house. A squirrel, frisking in a big tree beside the door, set up an indignant chatter at the interruption, a clamour which persisted until Cassel had gone inside.

Silence descended again, and he looked around, his face twisted with the same anger which had gripped him when he had first returned here the other day. This was desecration, wanton and deliberate. It would be better, he felt, to burn the whole thing to the ground. Yet it was no longer his to do even that with.

In the big parlour he crossed to the fireplace and examined the bricks. There had been a loose one, and he had hidden things behind it as a boy. He pulled it out, and drew out an old and battered top, left there through the years and forgotten. But no one else, apparently, had ever discovered that hiding-place.

He tramped from one room to another, looking into possible spots, but there was only ruin here. Upstairs it was not quite so bad. In his own old room, the door had been shut, and it was almost as it had been long since. He was standing there when the squirrel began its excited chatter again.

For full five minutes it kept it up, and yet there was no other sound, no sign of anything to disturb it. Carefully, alertly watchful now, Cassel moved. At the window, keeping well back out of sight himself, he viewed what he could see until it was all clear in his eyes, then made a circuit to the other windows upstairs. The squirrel was quiet enough now, somewhere a meadow-lark sang in the fields.

He was on the stairs when he saw what he had been looking for. A man, over near the doorway, crouching back in the shadows, waiting with a still patience worthy of a better cause. Proof that Cassel had been watched when he rode out of town. The man held a gun, but he had not seen Cassel. Apparently he had paid no attention to the chattering of the squirrel.

To his surprise, Cassel saw that this was Brager. He had supposed that the man was long gone from Bitter Creek, and finding him here and intent on ambuscade made his own voice brittle as he spoke.

'Brager,' he said. 'I warned you before to leave the country. By rights, I'd ought to kill you now. Mebby I will. Drop that gun!'

Brager did so, jerking as if stung. Cassel watched him with a sort of wintry humour. There was such lurking terror in the eyes turned to him as he had never seen before.

'But if I did, that would be murder, just the same as you'd planned,' Cassel went on wearily. 'And that don't give me much choice. So get out. And this time, keep travellin'. If we meet again, next time I reckon I'll have to finish you.'

Brager regarded him for a moment in sheer surprise. There was a strangely desperate, hunted look in his face which Cassel could not quite fathom. Then he scuttled out and was gone like a trapped creature released from its cage. He had come there to kill him, Cassel knew, and realized that he had probably been foolish to let him go, since that was the second time. And doubly so without searching him for an extra gun.

Cassel hurried down the stairs and to the door, and was in time to see Brager riding away through the trees and brush, and losing no time about it. And now there was stir and movement all about the place. Cattle were beginning to drift back here in ones and twos and threes, a sort of ritualistic habit at about this time of day. There was water here, of course, after grazing in the hills since dawn, and comfortable shade. And, in and around the house, comfortable places to lean and scratch, as the hairy, rubbed walls and doors attested had been much done.

A big steer, the Horseshoe brand moving and wrinkling on his straining hide, was bawling hoarsely and working off a bit of surplus energy by gouging his horns into the pile of rubble where the old milk house stood. While a cow, off at the side, watched him with complete indifference.

Cassel watched too, a tight impatience in him. He had helped with the work of building that foundation, years before, had been inordinately proud of the result. The steer raised its head, staring, as Cassel walked into sight. Then, tail in air, it was gone, bawling anew.

He had been heading for his horse, convinced that any search was hopeless, without more information. Now he stopped at a sudden thought, and, looking more closely at the old pile of rubble, saw something which gleamed in the sun, something which had apparently attracted the attention first of the steer and caused it to horn the pile as it had.

Tincup! His breath came a little faster. What more logical place for hiding something? And if a man used a tin cup, it was usually for a drink—and the water in the old milk house had been clear and cold—

He crossed to it, and saw that what the steer had been digging at appeared to be a piece of tin, a corner of it exposed as the stones had shifted a little. Pulling aside some of the stones now, with mounting excitement, he saw that it was a metal box. Perhaps a foot in length, by half as wide and a third as deep. Probably it had been placed in the middle of the wall before that had been broken down.

It was somewhat rusted, but still tightly shut and locked. Maybe it wasn't anything—but he had a hunch now that this was what Paddy had meant by staring at that tin cup on the wall.

A couple of strokes of another stone broke the rusted lock. And inside, he saw after only a brief examination, were Paddy's missing papers.

The wild ebullience of the steer had helped, this time. Cassel studied a few of the papers, and it was easy to see why there had been a truce between the two men, with this in Paddy's possession. Noting the steady rise of Robert Yoder, rightly interpreting his ambition to rule all of Bitter Creek, Paddy had quietly taken steps to checkmate him, and had been ready when the time came.

The first paper was in regard to Judd. A carefully-attested and witnessed story of a killing, which, in the hands of proper authorities, would send Judd to the hangman.

There were other papers, some of which affected Yoder much more personally and vitally. So long as these had been in Paddy's possession, Yoder had not dared to move against him. And, knowing Paddy as he did, it was probable that Yoder likewise had a stack of incriminating evidence somewhere in his possession, which had kept Paddy from any more than holding him in check.

Having glanced at two or three of the papers, Cassel slipped the whole package inside his pocket. They'd bear a lot of careful study, a little later. And Paddy would be mighty pleased that they had been found.

For he sensed that Paddy would at least want some of these papers used, now. He had reached a point, at Yoder's hands, where Yoder had no further power to hurt him. And there was irony again.

Cassel did not return directly to town. He had been too long a campaigner against a skilled and ruthless enemy. Brager had made tracks out of there in a hurry, but where he had gone, or whom he might have reported to, was a matter for sober conjecture. He might easily be somewhere between Tincup and Canyon, again patiently waiting in ambush.

Circling, taking his time, Cassel slipped into Canyon from the opposite direction, and made his way to the *Cattleman*. At the head of the stairs he encountered Doc Gray, and one look at the doctor's face told him that something was amiss.

'Paddy's dead,' Gray said shortly, and his face worked a little. He had never, Cassel knew, had much use for Paddy or what he stood for. In life, Paddy had been a ruthless boss, as bad in his own way as was Robert Yoder. Yet as an individual, Paddy had always been a gentleman, with a charm and gaiety which no one could deny, and it was that side of him that Doc Gray was remembering.

Cassel stared, shocked at the news.

'Dead,' he repeated. 'And I'm afraid it's my fault. I talked to him too long—I could see that he was overtired—'

'It's not your fault,' Doc interrupted harshly. 'It's murder. Take a look!'

He led the way, back inside the room, and

nodded shortly to where Paddy lay, just as he had been before, except that his eyes, which had been so expressive, the only really live thing about him, were closed now. But there was a gash on his head, and blood had dripped down it across the side of his head, on to his pillow.

A gash such as was just now beginning nicely to heal on Cassel's own skull. One made by the ripping stroke of a gun-barrel, smashing down. Cassel stared in dismay.

'But his guards!' he exclaimed. 'Quantrell—'

'That drunken loafer said he'd stepped out for just a minute, to get a beer across the street,' Doc said grimly. 'But it was long enough! Rusty's gone for a talk with him! Look here.'

He led the way to the window, and pointed. Down below, half-hidden in grass, lay a ladder, where it had been set up, against the window. The killer had climbed up to the second floor here, let himself in, had callously smashed Paddy over the head with his gun-barrel, then had let himself out again the same way.

'Somebody knew Quantrell's habits pretty well,' Cassel said grimly.

'Habits, hell!' Rusty had appeared in the doorway. His face was grim and tired, and there was genuine grief in it as he looked toward where Paddy lay.

'It was Horseshoe gold!' he rasped angrily. 'But he won't pull any more tricks, sellin' men out! He's dead, Marshal—I killed him. I'd ought to've guessed, after the way he was supposed to be watchin' the Merc, and let it burn. Look!'

He drew his hand out of his pocket, holding a ten-dollar gold piece.

'He'd just spent this for beer, over at the *Northern*,' he growled. 'And others like it, lately. And only Yoder pays off with gold, around here! I shoulda known before!'

Stonily, Rusty stared at Paddy, turned and tramped down the stairs again. The two men looked at each other, turned at a new sound. Kathleen came in.

'I heard what he said—and what you said, Doctor,' she said. 'That set me to thinking. I heard a sound back here, maybe half an hour ago. Just after Quantrell had gone across the street. I saw somebody going away, through the back yard, but I didn't suspect what had happened, then. I didn't see the ladder—'

'But you saw who it was?' Gray prodded.

'Yes,' she agreed. 'It—it was a man from Horseshoe. Brager, his name is.'

* * *

Brager! The thing was startling, half-incredible at first thought, then not so much so. He was working for Yoder, and Yoder was desperate now. And suddenly it was all clear to Cassel, with Quantrell's treachery explained.

Lounging back there against the walls, apparently half-asleep, the spy had been wakeful and alert. He had seen that Paddy was telling Cassel something, now that Cassel had found a way to talk to him. *And Paddy had known, then, but too late to tell, that the man was a traitor!*

That was why he had quit looking at Cassel, answering questions directly, had stared instead at the tin cup on the shelf! Quantrell had not gotten the significance of that, but he had realized the danger, had lost no time in communicating with his employer.

They had lost no time, in turn, in silencing Paddy completely and for ever. Quantrell's trip across for beer had afforded the opportunity and the excuse, but spending a gold eagle had betrayed him to Rusty.

Yoder had probably met Brager, running away after his failure to kill Cassel. Which argued that Brager was closely watched himself, that terror rode with him. Cassel could picture what Yoder would have to say at such a time. Needing another job done, he had given Brager another chance, and this was the result.

Cassel turned suddenly.

'Anticlea!' he exclaimed.

The others were at his heels, but

Kathleen's words were reassuring.

'Mother has been with her, all afternoon.'

Anticlea was sleeping, and there was no cause for apprehension there. Cassel went to his own room and, taking the package of papers from his pocket, put them away. Since Yoder did not suspect, or even have reason to suspect, that he knew the secret or would be able to find them, they would be safe enough.

He made a few preparations, and came out again, and encountered Kathleen in the lobby. She looked at him, a sudden anxious question in her eyes as she noted his equipment.

'You're going after Brager?'

'Of course,' he agreed. 'I'm the law—and this is the first time I've really had anything to do.'

'I suppose you must,' Kathleen agreed. 'But be careful, won't you? He—he's killed already, to-day. And he reminded me somehow of a cat gone wild, as he slipped away. You know—slinking and feline but awfully bad.'

'I know,' Cassel agreed, and did not bother to tell her just how dangerous a man Brager had suddenly become. He had been dangerous all along, of course, but up to then, it would have been useless to arrest him, with no judge, no law in town save himself. He could not arrest a man and judge him as well, and be the complaining witness against him.

Now it was different. It was Paddy, not himself, whom Brager had attacked this time, and things could be done in an orderly way, with public opinion in the judgment seat.

It was doubly important to get Brager now—partly because he had murdered Paddy, and Paddy had put Cassel in as marshal, given him his chance, here in Bitter Creek. But far more important was to bring Brager in and through him incriminate the man who was responsible for all that was happening here of late—the real killer. Yoder. For if Brager was like a tame cat gone suddenly wild, Yoder was like a dog gone mad.

CHAPTER NINETEEN

Inquiry revealed that Brager had been seen riding out of town just after the time of the killing. Two or three men had seen him go, but had thought nothing of it. One of them, standing in the doorway of the *Big Bottle Saloon*, questioned in turn.

'What do you want him for?' he asked.

'Murder,' Cassel said succinctly, and they asked no more questions, but watched him go in a respectful silence. In the last few days, Cassel had won the respect, if not the liking, of most of the community.

'Don't know what a one-armed man can hope to do against a killer,' one man commented. And another shrugged in turn, moving back to the bar.

'Looks to me like one arm's plenty, for him,' he said. 'I'd hate to have him after me, even if he didn't have *any* arms!'

Unaware of this appraisal, uncaring in any case, Cassel considered his own course. Brager had not taken the road to Horseshoe, but was swinging south instead. That might be only a ruse, after which he would strike back to the ranch, or again, with an uneasy conscience to dog his footsteps, he might suspect that he was already being followed. In that case, he could be heading for the wild country down on the edge of the Indian lands.

Cassel had had experience with men of Brager's type before. While a cold-blooded murder would not trouble their mind it gave them always an uneasy feeling of retribution dogging their heels. Such men would flee in a fear growing almost to panic, with no man pursuing except in their imagination.

If that was Brager's course now, he was choosing shrewdly, Cassel conceded. Hereabouts, and close to the settlements, there had been no Indian trouble for a long time. But off beyond was a big slice of country which the red men were determined to hold for themselves, and according to the several treaties granting them that territory in perpetuity. For white men to venture far into that section was to risk sudden and painful scalp trouble.

Somewhere in that nebulous no man's land between the two, Brager might hope to find sanctuary.

There was the consequent added risk of going that way after him, alone, and an added factor for Cassel to take into consideration. Brager would soon discover that he was on his trail, and would do his best to kill him, preferably from ambush. Brager would be carrying a rifle, which could outrange a six-gun.

But using a rifle was out of the question for Cassel. It was a revolver or nothing. Here he would have to depend on a greater skill than his opponent possessed, to carry him through. If he failed—well, what would be the difference.

Cassel had taken the precaution to fill his duffel-bag with provisions for a long trip. For a while, once he had left Canyon behind, the going was good, open country which offered little cover for an ambuscade, yet revealed tell-tale signs of the fugitive's passing. Twice, in the next hour, Cassel found hoofprints in open ground, and knew that Brager rode a shod horse, and that the right fore-shoe was a little loose. Likewise, there was an imperfection in the left hind shoe which was distinctive.

Half an hour before darkfall, a bullet came back warningly, from a dry wash which, cutting through the level ground and covered by the season's growth of grass, did not show from a hundred feet away. It was so close that there could be no doubt it had been meant to kill.

The range was a little long, however. Brager had been too nervous to wait until he was upon him. He emptied his rifle in a flurry of wild shooting, then, still out of revolver range, ran to where his horse had been hidden, and galloped away.

'A little more patience, and you'd have had me, cold turkey,' Cassel reflected. 'But your nerves are jumpy as a hungry flea, looks like.'

He followed until dark, but made no effort to travel when dusk settled. He had a pretty good notion of how Brager would react now.

The thing which puzzled Cassel was why Brager had chosen to become a fugitive, instead of heading back to Horseshoe and throwing himself upon its protection. That in itself was queer. He must have killed Paddy at Yoder's order, and Yoder should protect his own men—more particularly when they were successful.

There was a chill to the night which marked the far advance of summer. It wouldn't be long until the mountains would wear white again. Towards dawn, Cassel's arm throbbed and pained, and he awoke, cold but gripped in a sweating terror. He rolled over, and a bullet slapped the ground where he had been, and he kicked free of his blanket and felt for his own gun.

Cassel lay then, not moving, waiting for the next move. He gave a grudging admiration to Brager, not having believed that he would slip back and try any such trick as this. Kathleen had been right. The man was cat-like and wild.

His leg rubbed on a small stone, and he moved a little, laying his gun down carefully, picked up the stone and tossed it to the side, a small noise in the night. Nothing rewarded that effort, and then he heard the distant receding thud of horse's hooves. Knowing that his try had failed, Brager was too wary to make a fight of it where the odds were even. That wasn't his way of fighting.

Sunlight splashed up like sudden thunder, and the world it unveiled lacked even a glimmer of moisture on the now cured grass. Down this way was dry country, once the rainy season had ended. Even streams had a way of losing themselves in the thirsty earth. It was not desert, but that seasonal habit explained why no cattle ran here, nor even buffalo, once the rains were over.

Cassel knew this country of old, and he wondered how well Brager might be acquainted with it. A lot could depend on the answer. He found a small spring, which in another week would cease to flow, and filled his canteen, and his horse sucked greedily at the trickle of water until it was down to the mud.

He rode with the same untiring patience, not hurrying, finding an occasional sign of the passing of Brager. Now the country was becoming more broken, though there was no timber and little brush, save for an occasional patch of unedible, wild, currant-like fruit, growing beside a cluster of rocks. Sage reared now and again, starkly grey against a grey-brown landscape. The dried grass rustled underfoot, the faint powdery dust which they stirred was sharp and acrid when a small gust of wind blew it up at them.

Here was better cover for a hunted man who might turn hunter again, and Cassel resorted to new tactics, circling now and then, making use of the cover himself. Towards noon he was rewarded by sight of Brager, a quarter of a mile away and behind him. The killer had been hidden, watching the back-trail, waiting for Cassel to come along it, and had all but been surprised in turn. Now, like a startled prairie-chicken, he was scuttling to his horse and fleeing again, not even stopping to shoot back.

That suited Cassel well enough. Nervous tension was as good as a couple of extra deputies in this game. Brager was unsure of himself, and he would wear down faster than Cassel. And one question had been answered. He wasn't merely trying to escape. It was an obsession with him now, that Cassel must be killed before he could hope to make any final escape. That attitude presented its own problems, but it assured Cassel that he could keep in fairly close touch with the man he trailed until a final decision was reached.

There was a harried desperation beginning to show in the man. It might be slow in taking final shape, but this country would build it up as a swallow, daubing mud, builds a nest out of bits of nothingness. At most seasons of the year this would have been just another bit of wild country, shunned alike by Indians and whites for its inhospitality. But now it was more than that. Now it held the pressure of a closing giant hand.

At mid-afternoon, Cassel saw where Brager had found a spring, or what had been one, up to a few days before. There was still the trace of starved greenery below it, where for a while water had made a thin trickle, starting out bravely, then being swallowed as though it had not existed.

Now the spring was only a memory. With a new season, and snow soaking deep, it would flourish for a time. To-day Brager had been disappointed. So had his cayuse. It had pawed restlessly, bringing up traces of half-dried mud.

They were gradually climbing now. Close at hand the land had a flat look, but looking back, the slope was apparent, and there was more ahead. This was a sort of divide, though there seemed no reason for its being. Only here, as night drew on again, the air had the sharpness of a whetted knife.

Clouds rolled up in a black ball of fury and untangled like a rolling ball of yarn, lightning made a wild play across the horizon, seeming to come from above and to spread out below at the same time. The wind was an untamed virago, smashing out of the stillness, howling like a banshee. And a few big drops of rain, big as two-bit pieces, came in a flurry and were gone as quickly, leaving the earth drier than before. Then sudden stars shone from out the vanishing cloud-wrack.

Brager would have been hoping desperately for rain which would soak the grass, giving moisture for his horse; rain which would fill, for a few minutes at least, the low spots with water that a man could drink. The thunder had been unseasonably late, but it was only sound and fury.

Cassel found a little spring, that evening, and there was water in it—not much, but enough. He built a fire and let its beacon flare redly in the surrounding dark, and fried bacon and made coffee. Then he went well away from it and camped, and, an hour later, moved a second time, silently now and in an opposite direction. And now, as he slept, he held one end of the rope which tethered his horse attached to his own boot. A few times it bothered him during the night, but that was the only disturbance.

With the new day, he saw where Brager had found the spring and drank, but had failed to find him. Which attested to the nervousness of the man.

Despite the gradual rise in elevation, it was hot here under the sun, shining with a last fling of fury before it should thin its rays and withdraw sullenly to the south. There were flies here, too—little gnat-like creatures which rose up in swarms and made themselves a torment, and by them Cassel knew that he was close to the crest, even if the eye should be in doubt. Always they were here at this time of year, for a few miles, and then, a quarter of a mile beyond the invisible limit they had fixed for themselves, there would be none.

A man who did not know their habits, a man already raw in mind, could be driven half crazy by their swarming persistence.

Here were antelope again, indifferent to the gnats, seeming not at all troubled by the dry country. Fat and sleek and saucy, with a coyote prowling, not too hopefully, beyond them. Boulders studded the sky-line now—grey, massy rocks, some as big as rooms, which seemed to have been pushed up by an uneasy earth that had tried to absorb them and found the diet indigestible. Excellent country for a man who liked to set an ambush.

But Brager was not taking full advantage of his opportunities. He was discovering that, though he might know this country by any other season of the year, he was a tenderfoot hereabouts now. And tormented by the lack of water, by the fear of its increasing scarcity. The blazing sun overhead did nothing to help, and big rattlesnakes, torpid with languor, were driven back to seek the shade beside these massive boulders.

Cassel passed the line of them, a wild ridge running a quarter of a mile in width and endlessly to either side, and all at once the gnats were gone as well. Now there was a deceptive look of faint greenery beyond, though the country was much as it had been before.

That greenery promised water, but it was a mockery. But if there had been any doubt in Cassel's mind as to how Brager was faring, it was removed now. Water had become paramount in the outlaw's mind, above every other consideration. He was heading down here in the hope of finding it—and perhaps with the knowledge that, about a day's ride ahead, it was certain.

That far ahead was the Sink. It was a spot

where two or three springs made a joint pond which always held water, even through the driest seasons, and as such it had acquired a reputation. There would be water there, if not before.

And there would be none short of it, Cassel was certain. Both of them had to reach it now—and the man who got there first would hold victory in his hands. Victory, and life, and death. It was as simple as that, and as stark.

CHAPTER TWENTY

But this was what he had been counting on, and hoping for. That Brager, not knowing this country and its ways, would venture so far into the dry country that he would have to go on to the Sink. Now it was certain that he was heading that way and, wittingly or otherwise, he had fallen into the trap which Cassel had set for him.

It was doubtful if he realized yet how neatly Cassel had worked it. His circling, more than once, had been intended as much to turn the fugitive in the way he wanted him to go as anything else. Well, that part of the game had worked. The result was certain now, though the outcome remained in doubt. For, once he realized the trap, Brager would grow desperate and wild.

Proof of that was soon afforded. Brager came in sight abruptly, not two hundred yards ahead, and started to shoot. But he had allowed his nerves to play tricks on him. There was good shelter here, not only for Cassel but for his horse as well. He took to it, down in a small, brushless coulee, really a dry wash. And Brager, his sudden wild burst having gained nothing, rode on again. He wouldn't repeat that mistake again. It showed his state of mind, but his old caution would return now. He had been trusting to the superior range of his rifle alone. Next time he'd plan to make it really count.

And he had one advantage here. Cassel had to keep on his trail now. For who ever reached the Sink first had won, and Brager knew that just as well as he did.

Cassel used all his skill now to avoid traps, and twice in the next couple of hours he foiled attempts of the killer to catch him napping. And then, along in the afternoon, Brager's patience was rewarded. The rifle blasted suddenly, coming at a moment when the landscape ahead had seemed to offer no cover at all. It was that which had fooled Cassel, and even as he realized it, he knew that his horse had been hit and was going down, staggering to its knees, with a mortal wound.

He acted instinctively then, kicking his feet free of the stirrups, flinging himself off and down behind the cayuse as it collapsed. Brager shot twice more as it was going down, but none of his bullets touched Cassel.

Here was victory for him, however, if he could make full use of it. Even a half-victory would put Cassel afoot, and that would swing the odds all his way.

But Brager had been forced to pay a price for what he had won. His horse was nowhere in sight, which meant that he had ridden hard and gotten well ahead, then had left it hidden and crept back on foot, taking advantage of every bit of cover. With the superior range of his rifle for protection, he figured to get safely back to his horse again, whatever happened.

He moved now, and Cassel threw a quick shot which kicked up the dirt almost beside him, and Brager froze. The range was long for a revolver shot, but not too long. Withdrawing in the face of it, with hardly any cover behind, was not to his liking. Nor was fighting at fairly even odds a thing that the killer had any stomach for. Here he had overreached himself, failing to kill Cassel at the start.

It was certain that he wouldn't risk trying to get closer, making a final duel of it. Cassel squinted at the sun, and saw that it would be sliding behind the horizon in another hour. Unless he took action himself, Brager could be depended on to hold his position until night came to his rescue, then slip away.

With Cassel afoot, he would no longer worry about him.

For Cassel to move from the shelter of his dead horse would be even riskier business than for Brager. For Brager had the longer-range rifle. Still, it might be worked. The problem was which way to move, to the right or the left.

Brager's horse was hidden somewhere beyond. If he could outguess Brager and reach it first, he'd have the upper hand. But if he moved to the left and it was somewhere off at the right, Brager would have time to see what he was doing, once he was out of revolver range, and get to the horse ahead of him. Or if he moved right and the cayuse was off the other way, it would be just as bad.

It depended, in part, on the cover that Brager had been able to use in crawling back to his hiding place. Cassel lay, unmoving, for a full five minutes, studying the terrain. He couldn't afford to guess now. For if he did, and guessed wrong, it would be the last mistake he'd ever make.

Presently he had it. There was natural cover leading to where Brager crouched, from off to the left—and only from that direction. His decision taken, Cassel moved to the right, crawling, using all the skill he knew, reaching a point fifty feet to the right of where he had been before, and the shelter of a fair-sized rock.

From behind it, he fired a shot or so at Brager's hiding-place, and the rifle boomed angrily back, half a dozen times. When it had subsided, Cassel was already half-way back to the dead horse, crawling with even greater caution.

He reached the horse, and slung the duffel-bag over his shoulder. Crawling with it was more of a chore than when unencumbered, and the canteen, still half-full, persisted in getting in his way. But he had one advantage. Unless Brager saw through his ruse, he would be watching mostly off to the right, and was not apt to spot him here.

On the other hand, there was always the chance that Brager would try something new again. And one mistake, in such a game as this, could be enough.

By now, Paddy would be one with the other inhabitants of Boot Hill, not having lived to know that his papers had been found, or caring, any longer, what happened in Bitter Creek. But Paddy had worked to give him a square deal, and a chance, whatever his motive might have been. For that it was only fair that the man who had killed him should be taken.

Though there again was a big abstraction, and Cassel found himself speculating about it. Brager's intention had been what he had accomplished—murder, and the final, if tardy, silencing of Paddy. But probably it had been an act of mercy to a man hopelessly paralyzed, and Paddy, if he had had any say, would probably have been grateful for it.

★   ★   ★

Off at the side, the long silence was beginning to tell on Brager's nerves, just as everything had been doing for a long time back. He shut his eyes for a moment, tightly, against the long strain of watching, and tried to get a grip on himself, with the terse knowledge that he needed it. And as nothing moved, he flung another shot at that boulder, and watched, listening to the thin echo which came back.

Echo—and nothing else. His hand, moving back from the trigger, touched a bulge in his pocket, and he pulled it out and eyed it with bitter distaste.

A bunch of wadded-up bills—a thousand dollars. Blood money. Money, he knew deep in his heart, which was buying his own death.

He'd been a fool to go back and rook Robert Yoder out of this money, after Baby-Face had died in a vain effort to earn it. His attempt to give it back to Yoder had failed, and at every turn thereafter, when he tried to get off Horseshoe and out of the country, Yoder or one of the Horseshoe crew had turned up to check him. Sometimes it had not been a physical presence. But the terror of the man was so deep in Brager now that it had the same effect.

Discovering Cassel riding out to Tincup, Brager had been certain of success. How it had come about that Cassel had discovered him and warned him away, he had never been able to figure out. But that had raised his terror of the marshal almost to an equality with the fear he felt for Yoder, and he had firmly intended to take Cassel's advice and quit the country, then and there.

Instead, he had made the try, and had been stopped by Yoder, white with a cold fury that Cassel had escaped him. But Yoder had given him a new suggestion for earning the money which he had already been paid—a scheme so simple that there could be little risk in it.

He had demurred at first, pointing to the gun-guards, but had been reassured on that point. Then, with Yoder to goad him on, he had ridden into Canyon and killed Paddy. It had been simple, with Quantrell obligingly leaving the room unguarded.

Almost too simple. He had feared a trap, and the terror of it had dogged him with redoubled fears, the knowledge that he must get out of the country as Cassel had warned him. And then he had encountered Yoder again, who had suggested that he head this way.

'If Cassel does trail you, you'll have plenty of chance to get him, in such country,' Yoder had pointed out, and it seemed the sensible thing to do. Now, staring at the money, he wasn't so sure. All the Army of the Confederacy, it seemed, hadn't been able to kill Cassel in four years of shooting. He had a feeling that the man couldn't be killed.

Savagely he thrust the money back in his pocket, squinting at the sun. It was almost down. Another half an hour and it would be safe to move. He was cramped and stiff from lying so long in one position, taking advantage of such shelter as was here.

But he had played it safe to-day, and shrewdly. Now Cassel was afoot, and if he wanted to ride off and leave him, that was all that was necessary. He could escape with ease. And Cassel—any man on foot in this country now—would perish. His own tongue was dry and furry as he moved it in his mouth, his lips cracked. He'd have to get to the Sink, and fast. But it would be better travelling after sun-down.

His fears were beginning to quiet a little now—those jittery fears that had haunted him for days now. It was fear that had prevented him from ambushing Cassel somewhere, and he knew it. But he'd soon be all right now. He really had the upper hand at last.

He heard a sound, and swivelled his head around, and stared in open-mouthed, unbelieving surprise for a moment. From here, he could just see to where he had left his horse, hidden in a little draw, though it had been impossible for Cassel, from the point father beyond, to see it.

Or at least, Brager had figured it that way. He had studied the whole terrain carefully, forcing himself to a desperate calmness when setting his ambush. He knew he'd hidden the horse well. But the man must have eyes that could see through a brick wall. Somehow he had circled, had reached Brager's horse. Even as Brager looked, he was swinging up into the saddle, starting to ride away.

Mouthing frenziedly, Brager belatedly swung the rifle, shooting wildly. With the realization that it would do no good, that nothing would do any good against this one-armed man.

In that moment before he had started to shoot, Cassel could have dropped him easily in turn. Instead, he rode out of sight, and the new lease on life made Brager shiver with foreboding. For he knew now that Cassel intended to take him back alive—take him back to hang.

CHAPTER TWENTY-ONE

Cassel slept more peacefully that night. He drank some of the water still remaining in his canteen, poured the rest of it into the frying pan and held it for the horse to thrust its muzzle into it, watching the eagerness of the thirsty cayuse. It told him what he had been pretty certain of before. Brager would be in tough shape by the time he reached the Sink.

But he would probably reach it well enough. This was not like the hot, dry heat of desert country farther south. He would be able to travel, thirsty as he was.

Since it was his own purpose to reach it first, Cassel was on the move long before dawn. There had been a little dew this time, and a mist arose, a faint lifting blanket which weaved and shimmered as the pushing sun turned its searchlight toward the dark places. Full day had come when the horse snuffed the water and increased its pace without urging, and Cassel saw the Sink.

It was not much to look at. A small hill seemed to have pushed up there solely to give reason for two or three springs which trickled out from beneath brush and stones, and, at most seasons of the year, filled a pond down below to a depth of perhaps a dozen feet and a width of twice as much. It filled the pond and overran the side, and in spring and early summer made a sizeable stream for a mile or more before being lost. A few wilted-looking bushes still marked its course.

Now there was no stream, and the pond was only a mudhole near the bottom, trampled around the edges by the few animals which knew no better than to remain in this country through the dry season. One spring had ceased to flow. The other two were only trickles, and in the bottom of the Sink there was a scant half-foot of not too-inviting water. But the horse could scarcely be restrained at sight of it.

This was a remote spot, and there was little chance of anyone else being ahead of him. But Cassel held the horse back and had a look around, scanning the brush and rocks sharply. He could see nothing, and it would have been a physical impossibility for Brager, on foot, to be there ahead of him. He dismounted, and the cayuse plunged its head down and drank.

Thirst was a torment in Cassel's own throat now, the sun was gettng hot again. But drinking, for him, was not so simple. He could not stoop and scoop up water in his one hand very well. The best way would be to lie flat and stretch out, but even that was difficult, for here the level of the water had sunk sharply down, so that there was a considerable slope on every side.

He managed it, at a spot where the fresh water trickled down, cool and sweet, and had barely touched it with his lips when the gun broke the early morning stillness. Before its crash rang in his ears, Cassel felt the shattering impact of the heavy bullet striking him, knocking him off the precarious balance he had contrived, turning him over and around. It was like the kick of a mule, and fired from close range.

The bullet he realized in the next moment, had been aimed for his head, but it had hit his arm instead—or what remained of his right arm, the short stump below the shoulder. But the effect was the same.

He flopped and tumbled, and his feet struck in the mud and water down below, splashing it into the face of his cayuse so that it reared back, snorting. He was on his face then, fighting against the engulfing shock of pain, and he looked up the slope into the wolfish grinning face of Brager, raising his revolver for a finishing shot.

Surprise paralyzed Cassel for a moment. He had known that it must be Brager who had fired the shot, yet the thing, on the face of it, was impossible. But there he was, steadying for what remained, and it was clear that he had been here, had drunk, and had withdrawn well out of sight and waited for Cassel to arrive, to be off-guard and about to drink.

With his good hand, Cassel clawed for his own gun, and found the holster empty. It had slid out as he tumbled. Brager fired again, and Cassel knew a small wonder that he should miss at that range. But now he saw his own gun, where it had slid, and turned a little and his fingers closed on it, and this time their two shots blended as one.

Brager's bullet threw the half-baked mud of the Sink's rim in his face, and Cassel knew that his own had missed as well. But it had the effect of making Brager duck for cover, and the action steadied Cassel, with the first shock of his wound past. He shot twice more in quick succession, and wondered how he could miss so much. And then Brager's next shot came, and he felt the scratch of it on his cheek, as though a hot iron had been laid alongside it for a moment and then withdrawn.

Now, finding himself in a duel, the thing which he hated and feared, Brager was trying to crawl back to shelter where he could do this in his own way and at his leisure. With Cassel down below and no shelter, that would be the end, and knowing it, Cassel rose to his knees, emptied his gun, and knew that this time he hadn't missed.

He sank back, still half in the mud and water, astonished at his own weakness, cursing himself for it.

'Damned poor shooting!' he adjured himself. 'Empty a gun at that range to kill a man! What's come over you, anyhow?'

'Empty gun, eh?' the voice was casual, almost conversational, but it shocked Cassel so that for a moment he doubted if he had heard aright. And then he knew that this was no mirage, and understood the whole thing, seeing the scheme as though a curtain had been jerked aside. Yoder stood there, up above him, looking along a gun-barrel on which the sun glinted as cold as the steel itself.

He'd been wrong, all wrong, Cassel saw now, in figuring that he was herding Brager in the direction he wanted him to go. For it had been no matter of chance, nor design on his part, Brager coming here. Like other things, and completely under the dominating fear of Yoder, the man had done as he was told, with the hope that somewhere along the trail, he would succeed in killing Cassel.

But it was not Yoder's way to leave it to chance. So he must have ridden out this way himself to make sure with an agreement to meet Brager at the Sink. He had found Brager afoot, of course, had given him a lift as far as the Sink during the night, and then had left it to him to finish the job. Meanwhile standing by if anything went wrong.

'I never knew he was such a bungler,' Yoder said now, as though reading Cassel's thoughts. 'But he served his purpose. And I won't make the same mistake.'

His intention was clear enough. To kill Cassel and leave the two of them where they fell. If anyone ever chanced to find them, the assumption would be clear. Cassel had gone out after Brager, and had caught up with him here, and they had killed each other. No one would suspect Yoder of being the real killer.

He was taking his time now, since he knew that Cassel's gun was empty. And that it could not be reloaded while he watched. That was a chore for Cassel, under any conditions. He had to lay the gun on a chair or rock, and poke the shells in, one at a time.

'You've had a long string of luck,' Yoder went on. 'But you've stretched it to breaking. There's always a limit, you know.'

Cassel sat, regarding him impassively. His wounded arm pained and throbbed, but he said nothing. His silence seemed to infuriate Yoder. His voice rose, a little shrill with the passion which boiled in him.

'Well, why don't you say something?' he demanded. 'Maybe if you'd crawl up here on your belly, I'd still let you go—because of when we used to be boys together!'

'Get it over with,' Cassel said, a little wearily. 'You're just wastin' your breath now, and you know it.'

'Maybe I am,' Yoder admitted, and triumph rolled, a rich morsel, on his tongue. 'I guess I would kill you, all right, even if you crawled up here and kissed my boots. But I've always known that I'd get you to this point some day, and this time, you can't fight back.'

Cassel's fingers had been closing slowly on a handful of the mud. He brought his arm up and flung it suddenly, in one smooth sweep, and it struck Yoder full in the face, splashing across it like a smudge, and blinding him for a moment. It would give no real respite, Cassel knew, for he was too handicapped now to take advantage of it. But he snatched up a second handful of the mud and hurled it, and Yoder ducked, swiping a sleeve across his face to brush away the muck, and this time there would be no more delay.

But the bullet that broke the silence was not from Yoder's gun. It came from behind him, like a whip-lash in his ear, and Yoder spun around in sheer astonishment, and the gun in his own hand was lax. The astonishment grew to a blank wonder as he saw that it was Judd who stood there, a dozen short paces away, looking at him over his gun-barrel. Yoder's jaw sagged.

'Judd!' he said. 'You—what the devil?'

Judd's face was tired now, with a lined bleakness about it in which the dust had settled. But the gun he held was unwavering.

'You've got a gun, Yoder,' he said. 'Better use it. I'm going to kill you.'

CHAPTER TWENTY-TWO

Understanding came into Yoder's eyes, and a kind of cruel anticipation.

'So,' he said, 'it's on account of Rose, eh?'

'I guess it is,' Judd admitted. 'I've been tryin' to catch up with you for a long time to tell you. But you been hard to catch.'

He did not add that, Yoder being absent from Horseshoe, he had stopped long enough to give directions for the running of the ranch while both of them were away. That had been a last job to be done, for he was foreman of Horseshoe.

'You're a fool,' Yoder reminded him harshly, and knew that he was talking against the wind. He had seen this thing in Judd's face, back there in town. 'With me you have a good job—and between us we rule the country. And it's a little late to start playing Sir Galahad. You've too many notches on your gun.'

'I'll have one more,' Judd said.

'Then let's start even, if we have to kill each other off,' Yoder shrugged. 'We'll holster them and try it—since you're givin' me a chance.'

'I've been takin' your pay,' Judd said tonelessly, and slid his own gun into the leather. And in that moment, quick as a pouncing cat, Yoder whipped up his own gun and fired.

The bullet, a shade too fast for accuracy, took Judd in the shoulder and spun him half around, and slowed his attempt to drag his own gun again. Steadying then, Yoder's finger was on the trigger for the finishing touch, when Cassel's shot decided it. Yoder's bullet went wide, and he stood for a slow, uncertain moment, then his knees buckled and he went down like any lesser man who had never known power.

Judd turned, his face grey, his arm dripping blood which stained the gun he had finally managed to draw, and made it slippery in his hand. There was sheer amazement in his face as he looked at Cassel, now on his feet and climbing to the rim of the Sink.

'I thought your gun was empty,' he said.

'It was,' Cassel agreed. 'But while the two of you chewed the rag, I had time to get one shell in.'

'And you made it count,' Judd murmured.

'It never pays to stop and talk at such a time,' Cassel told him. 'Too many things can happen.'

Judd's gun slipped to the ground and lay unheeded.

'Reckon we can make out to tie each other up?' he asked.

'Nothin' like tryin',' Cassel agreed, and eyed him sharply. 'Your wound looks clean. Missed the lung, too, I guess.'

'It was high,' Judd nodded, his face tight with pain.

'And we've both bled enough to clean them—gives them a good chance to heal,' Cassel said mechanically.

They worked for a time in silence, assisting

each other to peel off Brager's shirt and to tear it to strips. It was a matter of each using a hand, rather awkwardly but to good effect, to bandage their wounds. Judd spoke finally.

'I never figured to be sidin' you in a show-down,' he said. 'But after what he wrote to Rose—and the way he aimed to treat his wife—' His mouth tightened. 'She'll be free now,' he said, and looked at Cassel speculatively. 'She found out, long back, she'd made a mistake.'

'Yeah,' Cassel agreed absently. 'Can you ride?'

'I'll have a try at it.'

★   ★   ★

They rode together, taking it easy for a common reason, both mostly silent. The red flush of fever was on Judd's face that night, but he was doggedly ready to ride again the next day. Both of them were weaving in the saddle when they reached Canyon in late afernoon, and it was Doc Gray who discovered them and called help, then had them carried up to beds in the *Cattleman*. It was, Cassel felt, an inglorious return.

'Be making a hospital out of this place next,' he groaned, and had a glimpse of Kathleen, and was asleep.

The next morning, despite Mrs. Kenney's protests, he felt better enough to insist on getting up and dressing. A little shaky, he looked in on Judd, saw Rose sitting beside him, and received a scowl in return.

'I'm weak as a starved calf,' Judd growled. 'And there you go prancin' around like a skittish cayuse!'

'He's peevish because he only had a little broth for breakfast, and he wanted a beefsteak,' Rose smiled. And Cassel, nodding, went out into the hall and down the stairs.

He stumbled on the lower stair, and caught at the railing, and would have fallen even then had not Kathleen suddenly been beside him, and eased him across to a chair.

'What are you doing, up and dressed?' she chided. 'You'd ought to know better!'

'Never did know much,' Cassel said, and found himself, unexpectedly, grinning in turn. 'And you can't teach an old dog new tricks.'

'Old dog!' she said indignantly. 'You look ten years younger—almost like a boy, with that great mass of hair off your face.'

Cassel didn't know what to say to that, so he said nothing. He closed his eyes for a moment, and when he opened them again he was alone. He felt aggrieved, and considered going on out and getting himself some breakfast, and felt too tired to make the effort. He was still sitting there when Kathleen re-entered the room.

'I was just up to see our patients,' she explained. 'It was time for Anticlea to have her medicine.'

'How is she?' he asked, without much interest.

'Didn't you look in on her? She's been wanting to see you. She's fine. The doctor says she can get up in a day or so.' Kathleen's voice was cool, and she did not look at him. 'I'll help you back up stairs, if you want to see her now.'

'I can walk by myself,' he growled.

'Then why don't you?' she demanded.

He shook his head stubbornly.

'I don't want to walk—or to see her,' he said. 'I'd a lot rather sit here. And I'm hungry.'

'That always makes a man short-tempered, doesn't it?' she said tartly, then with more contrition, 'I'm sorry. You've gone through a lot, I know. I'll get you something.'

She moved to do it, and he watched her in a sort of dreamy contentment, until she came to announce that it was ready. She gave him a hand to his feet, and into that cozy little private kitchen off the lobby, and he ate in silence.

'Everybody's talking about you to-day,' Kathleen said suddenly. 'They're all remembering when they used to know you—or pretending like they did, anyway. You're the big man in Bitter Creek again. But you don't seem much excited.'

'What difference does it make?' he asked.

'It should make a lot—everything considered,' Kathleen said. 'You've had a hard time, I know. But—but Anticlea is free now—and she long ago realized her mistake—'

'Do you think that I'd ask anybody to—to marry me now?' he demanded with sudden harshness. 'And me only half a man—a cripple?'

'Why not?' she retorted. 'You've proven yourself considerably more of a man than the best of them thought they were. Anticlea will take you quickly enough.'

He shook his head.

'I'm not such a fool as to ask any woman,' he said. 'In any case—she chose Yoder. That was that.'

'But if she still loves you—and realizes her mistake?'

'She did it with her eyes open. And opened mine in the process,' he said a little grimly. 'As for love—she's never known what it means. She means well,' he added, a little wearily. 'But she's too shallow to feel anything very deeply or for very long. She'll have Horseshoe, and Judd can run it.'

'You mean, you—you don't love her any more?'

'That's about the size of it,' he agreed glumly. He stood up, looking at the violin, and turned away so suddenly that he staggered. He clutched at a support, and then Kathleen had caught him, and he clung to her.

For a long moment they stood so, and he was conscious of the warm sweet nearness of her which had troubled him in his dreams and haunted him in his waking hours; of the strength in her arms, the faintly intangible perfume of her hair. He knew hunger which was like a pain, and turned again with sudden abruptness and she saw his face, and put her hand on his arm with sudden boldness.

'If you d-don't love her,' she said, 'then—why, if you'll not be a fool, why I—I'll have to be one, I guess. You've lost Tincup—but you haven't lost everything, you know. Don't—don't be a fool on account of your arm, Clyde!'

He looked at her then, a long, slow incredulous moment. And what he saw in her eyes his own softened, and then, using his arm to good purpose, he gathered her close.

'Do you mean you—you'd—will you marry me?' he asked. 'Though I've no right to ask you—a cripple—'

'You're a man,' she reminded him. 'My man now.'

Presently, and quite unexpectedly, he grinned, but this time with perfect contentment.

'Once Tincup's rebuilt,' he said, 'you'll

make a dream come true.'

'Tincup?' Kathleen looked at him, startled. 'But I thought—you'd lost it—'

'Didn't I tell you?' he asked. 'I found Paddy's papers. And took another look at them this morning. Among other things there was a mortgage—made out to the Bank of Canyon, by Dick Hawes, actin' as my agent, for Tincup. And duly paid and cancelled.'

His mouth tightened a little again.

'Paddy got hold of that someway, and it was what he used to keep Yoder in line with. Tincup never did belong to him! No wonder he burnt the Merc, anything, to try and destroy that paper!'

'And Paddy kept that—knowing—' there was distress in Kathleen's voice. 'I—I'm disappointed. I—I kind of liked him.'

'Paddy played square with his friends,' Cassel said quietly. 'There was a letter to me, explaining it. While I was away, and might not return, it served Paddy well to keep Yoder in line. And to square things up, he left me everything he had. Were you sayin' something about me being the big man in Bitter Creek, now?'

There was almost consternation in Kathleen's eyes as she looked at him now.

'All that?' she gasped. And flushed crimson. 'Oh, I—I didn't know. Now—you won't want me—I was just trying to make you see t-that Anticlea—'

'Don't try to get out of it, now,' he warned her. 'You got yourself into it—for a life-time job! And I'm all through with being a fool. When I get what I want, I hold on to it.'